The Prairie Dogs

The Prairie Dogs

Glenda Goertzen

Illustrated by Philippe Beha

Fitzhenry & Whiteside

Published in Canada by
Fitzhenry & Whiteside,
195 Allstate Parkway,
Markham, Ontario L3R 4T8

Published in the United States by
Fitzhenry & Whiteside,
311 Washington Street,
Brighton, Massachusetts 02135

www.fitzhenry.ca   godwit@fitzhenry.ca

10 9 8 7 6 5 4 3

National Library of Canada Cataloguing in Publication

Goertzen, Glenda
The prairie dogs / Glenda Goertzen; illustrations by Philippe Béha.

ISBN 1-55005-113-X
1. Dogs–Juvenile fiction. I. Béha, Philippe II. Title.

PS8613.O37P73 2004   jC813'.6   C2004-901308-4

U.S. Publisher Cataloging-in-Publication Data (Library of Congress Standards)

Goertzen, Glenda.
The prairie dogs / Glenda Goertzen; illustrated by Philippe Béha.
–1st ed. [164] p. : ill. ; cm.
Summary: Pierre used to be a show dog. Now he travels with three new friends,
answering to no human, enjoying a free and easy life, trying to stay out of
trouble. But trouble comes looking for him, and before long Pierre and his
friends are head-to-head with the bull dogs.
ISBN 1-55005-113-X
1. Dogs – Fiction – Juvenile literature. I. Beha, Philippe. II. Title.
[F] dc22   PZ10.3.A266 .G647Pr 2004

Fitzhenry & Whiteside acknowledges with thanks the Canada Council for the
Arts, and the Ontario Arts Council for their support of our publishing program. We acknowledge the financial support of the Government of Canada
through the Book Publishing Industry Development Program (BPIDP) for our
publishing activities.

Design by Fortunato Design Inc.

Printed in Canada

TABLE OF CONTENTS

1
Royalty in Silvertree

PRINCE PIERROT RUDOLPHE IV
L'ORGUEIL DE MONTREAL

THE WORDS WERE EMBOSSED in elegant blue script across the side of the motor home that lumbered into the parking lot of the Silvertree Gas 'n' Go. The customers of the small town's largest cafe peeked through the blinds at the man and woman who stepped out of the motor home.

The woman turned and leaned back through the side door.

"*Non*, Pierre," she said coldly. "It's far too hot for you to go outside. You would die of heatstroke, or cut your feet on the broken glass that I'm sure is strewn all over this parking lot. Use the privy like we showed you."

As she closed the door, the motor home's third occupant jumped onto the wide dashboard and slumped across it with a sigh. This passenger was a handsome young fellow, his curly black hair styled in the latest fashion, his slim nose sporting a distinguished moustache. He stood a good fourteen inches tall at the shoulder, an excellent height for his age.

"Nice looking poodle," observed the young pump attendant who came over to refuel the princely vehicle. "He looks kind of depressed, though."

"He ought to be," the woman snapped. "He had a chance to be a champion and he ruined it. 'His heart wasn't in it,' the judges said."

"He's a show dog?"

"An agility dog. We breed our miniature poodles to be show dogs, but Pierre's unusually large hind legs would disqualify him. They do give him an advantage as an agility dog—he's a terrific jumper. Only two years old and he's already won a shelf full of trophies. He went all the way to a national competition in Vancouver. He could have won the title of Agility

Master, and had his picture on the new bag of Crunchy Nibbles. We had high hopes for him."

"We still have high hopes for him," her husband said. "Another major competition is coming up in two months. We'll double his training. We'll isolate him from the other dogs in our kennel. They distract him. That's why he lost the competition— he kept looking at the other competitors."

"Maybe he's, you know, burned out," the attendant said as he plugged the pump nozzle into the gas tank. "Like pop stars who've been on tour too long. Maybe he just needs some fun."

They stared at him as if he had gone mad.

"He's a dog," the woman said. "What he needs is more discipline."

She walked toward the cafe, flapping the neck of her white silk blouse for ventilation. Her husband followed.

A skinny Chihuahua and a scruffy red terrier trotted into the parking lot. As they passed the motor home they stopped and looked up at Pierre. He sat up and stared back. He had seen a lot of the world through the bug-splattered windshield, but he had never seen dogs running loose out of doors with no humans in control. What would it be like to have that kind of freedom?

Suddenly the side door of the motor home opened a crack, and an eye peeked through it. The door opened wider to admit the head of the pump attendant.

"Hey, little buddy. Tough life, huh?" He extended a hand to Pierre, who drew back suspiciously. "Hey, I understand. You don't get many chances to make friends, do you? Hang in there, little guy." He withdrew and shut the door.

Pierre's ears perked up. The door hadn't caught. He jumped down and nudged it. It swung open. A moment later he was out the door and standing in the parking lot.

The heat was a shock after the drippy-nose chill of the motor home. "The humans ought to do something about this," he thought, lifting one burning paw after another. "They should fix the air, too. Careless of them to let it get so hot."

He looked around for the two small dogs, but they had disappeared. The pump attendant had gone back into the Gas 'n' Go. It occurred to Pierre that if he put his nose to the ground, he could follow the scent of the two dogs and perhaps catch up to them. Pleased with himself for inventing this clever new procedure, Pierre applied his nose to the baking pavement and followed the fresh scent into the shady alley that separated the service station from the small movie theatre next door. Pierre, of course, had no knowledge of movie theatres, and the jungle sounds from the matinee that was playing gave him an ominous feeling.

As he disappeared, the pump attendant came back outside. Noticing the open door, he guiltily slammed it shut, topped off the gas, and went back into the Gas 'n' Go.

Pierre paused to paw and sniff at the litter and smelly garbage bins, as curious as any elegant young prince who has never seen a junkyard. The steamy aroma from the back of the cafe made him drool like a Saint Bernard. It smelled a lot tastier than Crunchy Nibbles, the only food he had ever been allowed to eat. Suddenly Pierre *hated* Crunchy Nibbles. He hated the motor home, he hated the agility trials, he even hated his humans.

Guilt quickly smothered the hate. His humans took good care of him. Sure, they pushed him hard, but only because they wanted him to be a winner. He would do his best to win the next championship and then they would forgive him and everything would be right again.

A growl from halfway down the lane reminded him of the trail he was following. The growl was joined by several more, with a few barks and snarls thrown in. They seemed to be coming from the back of the theatre. Tail wagging, Pierre trotted forward, thrilled at the chance to introduce himself to common dogs who didn't belong to a kennel or the show ring.

He poked his head around the corner of the theatre.

There was the red terrier, backed against the wall by a large, bowlegged bull terrier. He was the toughest-looking dog Pierre had ever seen, all bone and bulging muscle stuffed into a scarred white hide. His broad muzzle peeled back to display a crowded collection of sharp teeth. Between those teeth was a dead Chihuahua.

"Let him go, Bull," the red terrier growled.

"I warned you two to stay away from the bins in our territory," the bull terrier rumbled around a mouthful of Chihuahua.

"Since when has this been part of your territory?"

"Since now. We've expanded."

Pierre trotted up to the dogs. "Sorry to interrupt, but I heard your discussion and thought maybe I could help negotiate—"

"This is none of your business, puffball." The bull terrier took a few stiff steps toward him, the Chihuahua swinging limply in his jaws. The tiny dog's paws twitched. It wasn't dead, just unconscious. "Take off before I sneeze and blow you across the highway."

Pierre decided to overlook the insult. You couldn't expect proper etiquette from a common unleashed dog. "What are you doing with that Chihuahua?"

"We figured we'd play with the little rat for a while and then give what's left of him back to Dare here."

As the dog spoke, several others crept into view from behind garbage bins, fences and clumps of tangled weeds. They didn't look very clean, and they didn't look very friendly. Pierre could see his negotiating skills would be useless here, so he sat down and yawned.

A couple of the dogs yawned back. The bull terrier glared at Pierre, his nostrils twitching. Pierre yawned again, wider this time. Now all the dogs yawned, except for Bull, though it was a struggle for him—his muzzle trembled and his eyes watered.

Pierre threw back his head and yawned once more, throwing his entire soul into it—eyes squeezed shut, ears stretched back, tongue-tip curled, jaws gaping wide as they would go. Bull could no longer resist. He joined the rest of his pack in a hearty yawn, and the Chihuahua slipped out of his mouth.

The little red terrier was ready. She darted forward the moment the Chihuahua thudded to the ground. Grabbing him by the neck, she dragged him through a gap in the nearest fence while the other dogs were still helplessly yawning. They tried to follow, but none of them was small enough to slip through the boards of the fence.

"Just what do you think you're doing, puffball?" Bull's voice was a soft growl as he turned to face Pierre.

"Wagging my tail," Pierre answered cockily. As soon as the dogs recovered from their surprise, they would all have a good laugh over falling for such a simple trick. "As a rule, I don't usually notice I'm doing it. That's the problem with having a cropped tail, it's too short to keep track of. I once met a Doberman guard dog who said he couldn't scare away intruders because all the time he was trying to look fierce, his tail stump kept wagging away. A long-tailed dog, of course, would catch a glimpse of it in the corner of his—"

"You're going to wish you had wagged your miserable excuse for a tail in someone else's territory, puffball," the bull terrier interrupted. He and his pack didn't look like they planned to laugh anytime soon. Pierre hadn't noticed until now just how *large* they were.

"You're being rude," he pointed out, backing nervously against the theatre. "I'm a visitor to your town. How about an apology?"

"Scratches!" their leader barked. "Mug! Digs! Slasher! Chew him up!"

The dogs rushed at Pierre with scrabbling paws and flashing white fangs. Pierre dodged past them and raced down the alley, crying, "Your manners are shocking! I am Prince Pierrot Rudolphe the Fourth, Pride of Montreal, Champion of Quebec, and a Very Good Dog!"

The dogs didn't seem at all intimidated by his fame. He tried to throw a quick yawn over his shoulder, but it had no effect. Moments later he arrived at the end of the alley—the wrong end, an end blocked off by fences too narrow for even a poodle to squeeze through.

Fortunately, Montreal had good reason to be proud of Pierre. When he put his mind to it, no dog could beat him in an agility trial. He sailed over hurdles like a little deer, dashed through tunnels like a rabbit, and whipped through the weave poles like a snake with its tail on fire. As the snarling dogs closed in on him, he ran straight at them, jumping over their backs, ducking under their bellies, weaving between their legs—back and forth and around and around until they tripped over themselves and snapped at each other in confusion.

The bull terrier, not so easily bamboozled, singled Pierre out of the tangle of dogs and lunged at him. Pierre leaped straight into the air, sailed over the dog's head and onto his back. From there he bounced to the ground. He dashed down the length of the alley and around to the front of the Gas 'n' Go, where the motor home—

—was gone.

2
Beggars

PIERRE RAN ACROSS the empty parking lot and stopped at the edge of the highway. The motor home was lumbering down the road, slowly, but picking up speed. He stretched into a run. Cars whizzed past him, honking and swerving, but he paid no attention. The motor home grew smaller and smaller. He ran until his legs gave out, then collapsed at the side of the road. The motor home shrank into the distance until the prairie swallowed it up.

For a moment he just lay there, overwhelmed by the unbroken blue sky, by the unfamiliar scents of spicy grasses and wildflowers, and by the silence. For the first time in his life, he could not smell or hear a single human. Terrified, he scrambled to his feet.

"I'll go back to where they fed the motor home," he panted. "They'll come back when they notice I'm missing." Unless they abandoned him, because he was no longer a champion? He gave himself a good shake, to get rid of the road dust and the sinking fear. Then he limped toward the shade thrown by an old poplar whose heavy branches stretched across the ditch. It was the only tree he could see for miles in this grassy desert. He just had to get out from under all that sky for a few minutes.

As he pushed through the thick green grass that filled the ditch, he stopped in surprise. A fuzzy black-and-tan puppy drowsed at the foot of the tree. When she opened her eyes and saw Pierre, she hissed and sprang at the trunk, clawing at the rough bark. Pierre couldn't believe it—she was trying to climb the tree. She reached a height well above his head before she lost her grip and fell with a yip on her rump.

"Back off, dog, or I'll claw your ears right out of your head!" the pup growled, waving a fluffy paw at him.

"Calm down, pup," Pierre said. "I won't hurt you."

"Don't call me *pup*."

"Then what should I call you?"

She made a high-pitched sound that ruffled his ears. "*Mew*."

"Mew?" he echoed doubtfully.

"You're not saying it right, but close enough."

"I'm Pierre. How did you get here, Mew?"

"I wanted to see what a town looked like, so I ran away from the farm. Mother followed me and started to carry me back, but when we crossed the road one of these galloping tractors knocked her down, so now she's having a nap."

While she spoke the pup carefully licked every inch of her dusty fur and rubbed her paw over her face. Pierre looked around for the pup's mother, but found only a gray cat stretched out on her side among the wildflowers in the ditch. He smelled no breath and heard no heartbeat.

"I don't see your mother, Mew," Pierre said. "Just this poor cat."

"That's Mother."

"I think the hot sun has confused you, pup—"

"I'm not a pup!"

"Then what are you?"

"A kitten."

"Of course, how silly of me not to notice." Pierre backed away and stretched his nose into the wind, testing her scent for rabies or some other disease that might make a dog crazy. Her fur carried many scents, most of which he didn't recognize, but she smelled mostly of cats. The sooner he got this strange pup back where she belonged, the better. "What farm did you come from, Mew?"

The pup cocked her head in surprise, as if she hadn't realised the world contained more than one farm.

"The one with the barn," she said finally.

Pierre could see the distant barns and houses of four farms. The longer he stared, the farther away they looked. She would never find her way back without his help, but it would be just his luck to have his humans come back while he was wandering around the countryside with this crazy pup.

"Mew, come into town with me. I'll look after you."

"I can't leave Mother!"

When Pierre was a pup, one of his littermates had died. His mother told him and the other pups about the Forever Field, the sunny, peaceful haven for the spirits of animals who have left their bodies. Feeling sad and grown up, Pierre now passed the story on to Mew. Mew's mother, he explained, had moved on to the Forever Field even though she didn't want to leave her pup ("Kitten," Mew corrected) alone.

"Can Mother see me from there?" Mew asked.

"Animals can see everything from the Forever Field," Pierre said.

Mew went over to the cat and tried one last time to wake her. Finally she said, "I'm going away with Pierre, Mother. He's nice, even if he is a dog."

Pierre led her along the soft grass at the edge of the highway. Mew trotted after him for about a quarter of a mile, then tuckered out and sat down, whimpering. Pierre sighed and picked her up by the scruff of her neck. She was heavier than she looked. Halfway to town he dropped her and sat down to rest his aching jaw and burning feet. A flicker of movement across the highway caught his eye. A small animal watched them with shiny black eyes, sitting straight and still as a road sign. Then it flicked its tail again.

Pierre supposed he ought to chase it, but he was too tired to do more than give a half-hearted sniff in its direction. In the field behind it lay a collection

of holes in mounds of bare earth. Shy little heads bobbed up here and there to take a peek at the dogs. Whatever the animal was, there was a whole community of them right here beside the highway.

"What is that?" he asked.

"A prairie dog," Mew answered. "They're very rare, Mother says, so we shouldn't try to catch them."

"If that's a dog, then I'm a—" Pierre jumped as the shadow of wide wings and a sharp beak fell over them. He crouched protectively over Mew, but the shadow swept past them and across the road.

"A hawk!" said Mew, and let out a sharp yip. The prairie dog did a neat backflip right into its burrow and the hawk's talons snapped closed on empty air. It gave an angry shriek and wheeled toward the dogs, probably wondering if a real dog would be as tasty as a prairie dog. Pierre snarled, startling himself with the unfamiliar sound. The bird lifted away in search of easier prey.

Pierre ran the rest of the way into town with Mew dangling from his mouth. Even the birds were dangerous in this bizarre land where rodents thought they were dogs and dogs thought they were cats.

Back at the Gas 'n' Go he flopped down in the shade near the cafe door and licked his sore paws. Mew fell asleep against his side. Pierre looked down at her, thinking about Duchess. Duchess was a poodle from his kennel who had died giving birth to two chocolate-colored pups. Their humans had given the pups to another poodle, Koko, to raise along with her own new litter. Mew must have been adopted by a cat after her real mother died. How strange, though, that her new mother never told her she wasn't a kitten!

An hour passed, and another. Their patch of shade shortened as the sun swung across the sky. When the first hot rays crept over them, Mew woke.

"I'm hungry!" she whined.

Pierre had been hungry for some time, and he was annoyed that none of the humans around here had done anything about it. At home, when his stomach growled, a human automatically appeared with a bowl of Crunchy Nibbles.

"I guess we'll have to find our own food." The idea shocked him, but there was no getting around it. "Are you weaned, Mew?"

"Of course," she said haughtily, as if her puppy-hood was far behind her. "I've been eating slops for days and days now."

Pierre assumed "slops" were what passed for food on the farm. He stood on his hind legs and looked through the front window of the cafe. His nose told him all the food they could want was in there. When a customer came outside, Pierre and

Mew slipped through the open door. They trotted into the busy cafe, their claws clicking briskly on the tile floor. Heads turned and fingers pointed.

"Look at all the humans! There were never this many humans on the farm." Mew spun in circles trying to see everyone at once.

Pierre approached one of the tables, sat down, raised his front paws and gazed at the humans with his big brown eyes. Mew gave it a try but lost her balance and toppled over backwards.

"Aw," their audience sang. A woman who looked like she might have many grandchildren took a piece of hamburger from her plate and offered it to Pierre. He licked his lips and reached for it, but his teeth snapped closed on empty air as he was seized by the scruff of his neck. A large hand lifted him

into the air until he was eye-to-eye with a scowling young man wearing a white shirt and a tie.

"Whose dog is this?" the man demanded loudly. The humans stared guiltily at their plates. He marched over to the door and dropped Pierre outside. A few moments later the door opened again and a hand dropped Mew beside him.

"When do we get the food?" Mew asked.

"How dare he!" Pierre growled. "He tossed me out like trash! Me, the Pride of Montreal, the—"

"I'm hun-greee!" Mew howled.

"All right, all right. Come on, we might have better luck at a house." At the edge of the parking lot Pierre stopped. What if his humans came back while he was gone? Mew grabbed his ear in her teeth and pulled, shivering and whimpering as if she were seconds away from dropping dead of hunger. With a shake of his head to free his ear, Pierre followed her out of the parking lot.

Pierre had never known such hardhearted humans could exist in the world. No matter how hungry, mournful and adorable he tried to look, every door he scratched on closed on his face. One sour old man even swept Pierre off his porch with a broom. If Mew had stayed beside him he might have had better luck, but every time the door opened she ran and hid, muttering, "Farm cats never scratch on the door, that's a rule."

Pierre's impressive brain sprang into action. "I'll bet the humans around here leave food and water outside for their dogs like my humans do at home. Someone might share with us."

He entered an alley that separated two rows of houses. Sure enough, when he peered between the slats of a fence behind one of the houses, he saw a collie dozing beside a bowl overflowing with dog food. Pierre sniffed the air and wrinkled his nose in distaste. Crunchy Nibbles.

"Don't run away this time, Mew," he instructed.

"Try to look sad and hungry. No, don't roll your eyes around like that! You look like you have rabies. Soulful, that's what we're going for here."

He squeezed under the fence and strolled into the yard with Mew scampering behind, trying to look soulful. "Excuse me, but would you be so kind as to—"

"Out!" the collie barked, lunging to her feet and bounding toward them. "Out of my yard! Keep away from my house and my grass and my trees! Out-out-out!"

Pierre snatched up Mew, scrambled back under the fence and ran. He stopped halfway down the alley, wheezing. Mew was making that strange hissing sound again and her stubby tail was puffed out like a brush.

"How rude!" Pierre huffed.

"Shhh!"

A tiny face framed by butterfly-wing ears popped out of the honeysuckle bushes that lined the border of another yard. Pierre and Mew jumped back, startled.

"Quiet!" The Chihuahua glared at them with huge, glistening eyes. "Her life absolutely depends on it."

The little face withdrew and disappeared among the yellow blossoms. Pierre and Mew looked at each other, then plunged into the bushes and out the other side.

3
And Thieves

THE CHIHUAHUA CROUCHED in a bed of snapdragons on the other side of the bushes. All Pierre could see of him were the trembling tips of his ears poking up above the pink and red blossoms. He jumped and gave a squeaky yelp when Pierre and Mew joined him. He looked a little scuffed from his ordeal behind the Gas 'n' Go, but at least he was conscious now. Whispering again for them to be quiet, he stared toward the house with an expression of wild-eyed terror.

An enormous dog lay asleep on the lawn near the house. It was a fawn-colored Great Dane, one of the largest breeds in the world. Pierre was relieved to see a heavy rope attached to his thick leather collar.

"If he scares you so much, why don't you just leave?" Pierre whispered to the Chihuahua.

"Shhh!"

Something stepped out of the shadow of an apple tree. It was the little red terrier from the Gas 'n' Go. She crept toward the sleeping Dane and the meaty steak bone that lay in the dish beside the dog's head.

"She must be the bravest dog in the world," Mew whispered.

"Or the stupidest," Pierre added.

"For the last time, *shhhh*!"

The little thief was a few steps away from her target now. She eased past the giant head, freezing when the Dane twitched an ear. Her own ears quivered with excitement. The curly tufts of fur at their tips made them look a little like curved horns. After a moment she inched up to the bowl and sank her teeth into the bone.

"She's going to make it!" Pierre thought, and then, "No, I guess not." One of the Dane's eyes had opened. He was watching the little dog trying to tug the heavy bone out of the bowl.

"Run, Dare!" The Chihuahua's high-pitched yelp nearly split Pierre's eardrums. His companion was so startled she fell over backwards with the bone on top of her. The Dane lumbered to his full height with a thunderous bark. The little dog righted herself and tore across the yard with the half-chewed bone still in her mouth and the Dane snapping at her scruffy tail. Just when it seemed she was about to become a half-chewed bone herself, the heavy rope jerked the Dane to a halt. He flipped onto his back with a thud that shook the bumblebees out of the snapdragons. The smaller dog skidded to a stop, sauntered back to her pursuer, sat down just out of reach and chewed on her prize. The big dog

strained at his rope, clawing deep furrows in the grass. He snarled like a lion and bayed like a mad wolf, and the little dog went right on eating.

Suddenly she noticed the newcomers. She picked up the bone and carried it over to them, but not before kicking a little dirt in the Great Dane's face. He sneezed and glared at them as if he were planning a four-course meal and wondering what order to eat them in.

The Chihuahua had fainted. The other dog nipped his ear to wake him.

"What's the idea letting these two in, Mouse? They could have ruined the whole mission," she growled around her bone as the four of them pushed through the honeysuckle and into the alley. Then she took another look at Pierre. "Oh, it's you! Hey, Mouse, this is the mutt who saved you from becoming Bull's chew toy."

She circled Pierre a few times, sniffing him in a very forward manner. Pierre didn't sniff her back. She smelled like she'd never had a bath in her life. She had a lot of nerve calling *him* a mutt. She wasn't even a purebred, just a jumbled mixture of terriers with possibly a bit of dachshund thrown in. Pierre had never met a mongrel dog before, but he'd heard they were not very intelligent, and prone to insanity. Judging by what he had just seen, the rumor was true.

31

The Chihuahua didn't seem to care that Pierre had saved him from a grim fate. "Titan almost got you this time, Dare," he scolded. "You just about scared the worms out of me!"

"Aw, Mouse, a cranky butterfly would scare you."

Dare approached Mew, but the pup hissed and batted the terrier's nose with her paw. Dare was so startled she dropped her bone.

"Why did you steal that dog's supper?" Pierre asked. "Doesn't your human feed you?"

"What human? I've been on my own since I was old enough to leave my mother. Why the shocked look, Curly? You never met a stray dog before?"

"No," Pierre admitted.

"I should have guessed you don't know anything about life on the streets. You look like you've never even been on a street. Circus poodle, right?"

Pierre's hackles rose. "I am Prince Pierrot Rudolphe the Fourth, Champion Agility Dog."

"And I am Daredevil the First, Expert Scent Collector, Professional Chaser, and Master Thief. Dare for short. What are you doing here?"

"My humans drove away and accidentally left me behind in your dusty little dump of a town."

"Ah," the terrier said knowingly. "Happens all the time. Tell him, Mouse."

The Chihuahua's ears drooped. "Back when I

was called Chico, my humans moved out of our house one day. They packed up everything in boxes, even me. They threw me out of the car onto the highway and drove away. I would have died if Dare hadn't come along. She's been looking out for me ever since."

"Anyhow, Curly, you're better off without your humans," Dare said. "Just look what they did to your poor tail."

"There is nothing wrong with my tail," Pierre snapped. "They just shortened it a little, that's all—Mew! Oh, no!"

The pup had wandered back through the bushes and into the Great Dane's yard. Pierre could see her wriggling toward the giant dog with her chin in the grass, in imitation of Dare. He shot through the bushes and across the lawn just as the big dog noticed her. Pierre snatched up the pup and broke his own speed record getting out of the yard with the snarling Dane inches behind him. He crashed through the honeysuckle, dropped Mew between the other two dogs and collapsed, trembling.

"Not bad, Curly!" Dare approved. "Next time slow down a little, to make it more exciting."

"For the eleventh time, I'm *hungry*," Mew whined wearily.

"You have to be a pro before you can take on Titan, pup."

"Don't call me a pup! I'm a kitten."

"It's a long story," Pierre panted to the astonished terrier.

"Well, don't get any ideas about eating Mouse, kitten. Come on, we'll find you some dinner."

Still carrying her steak bone, Dare took them behind another house, where she crept into the garden and dug up a small carrot.

Pierre wrinkled his nose. "Dogs don't eat carrots."

"Why not? Afraid of a few specks of dirt? I suppose you city poodles have your food served at the dinner table, with napkins around your necks."

"It's stealing!"

"The humans will never miss it. Anyhow, they always blame the rabbits." Dare gave the carrot to Mew and flopped down in the shade to gnaw on her bone.

Pierre set to work digging up more carrots. If the kennel poodles could just see him now, digging in actual dirt and finding his own food instead of waiting for humans to provide it... He felt wild and dangerous.

Mew scampered around digging happily in all the wrong places. Then suddenly she tumbled into one of her holes and fell asleep with her fuzzy tail sticking up in the air. Pierre was surprised to see the sun setting already.

"I'd better get back to where my humans left me," he said.

Mouse jerked his head out of one of Pierre's holes. A fat earthworm dangled from his mouth like a strand of spaghetti. "The service station? But that's Bull's territory!"

"I have to be there in case my humans return tonight."

Mouse stared at him with wide, anxious eyes. Even Dare looked worried, but she only said, "Suit yourself, Curly. Here, Mouse, the rest of the steak is yours."

The two strays trotted away, the little Chihuahua staggering under the weight of a bone almost bigger than himself. Pierre carried Mew back to the service station. A crumpled old car stood at the edge of the parking lot. Two of its tires were flat and its windshield was a spiderweb of cracks. He wriggled through a bent rear door and stretched out on the cracked vinyl seat where he could see the highway through the door. They should be safe in here.

"Where are we?" Mew murmured sleepily. "Uh oh, we're in a car! Farm cats can't ride in the car, that's a rule."

"It's all right, Mew, this car won't be moving for a while," Pierre said. Mew curled up between his paws and went back to sleep. Pierre watched the sun sink into the horse pasture across the highway. He silently begged it to stay up in the sky, but it dropped so fast he was surprised it didn't bounce when it hit the horizon. When the first star poked through the blue velvet twilight, Pierre sighed, laid his chin across Mew's warm back, and closed his eyes. The muffled screams and explosions from the movie theatre next door chased him into his dreams.

When he woke, the stars had been swallowed by thick clouds that crackled and boomed. Something was crawling across the seat toward him. He snapped at it.

"Cut it out! It's me, Dare." The little terrier nosed him urgently. "You have to hide. The Bull Dogs are looking for you."

"The bulldogs?"

"They aren't really bulldogs, Bull just calls them that. They're his pack, the meanest, toughest collection of mutts in town. Even Titan doesn't frighten them."

Pierre shivered, picturing that vicious bull terrier and his pack hunting the dark streets for him.

"You need to hide. Follow me." Dare darted away. Pierre picked up Mew, who only blinked, yawned and went back to sleep.

Dare led him right across town. She slunk through shadowy alleys, under thorny hedges, and even through muddy drainpipes that ran under the streets. They were in one of these concrete tunnels when the storm broke, dumping heavy sheets of water upon the town. The dogs nearly drowned before they could scramble out of the pipe. Mew, of course, slept through the whole ordeal.

Dare glared at the flickering sky. "I hate rain! I've been collecting scents for weeks, and now they're all washed away. Today I found a dead robin to roll on. It was good and moldy, too."

"Your fur could do with fewer scents," Pierre muttered.

"And yours could do with a few more. You're the most scentless dog I've ever sniffed. Humans and soap, that's what you smell of."

Dare's final destination was a small brick building on the outskirts of Silvertree. Hopping through an odd fence of tall wooden wheels wired together, she led him around to the back of the building.

"It's called a museum," she said. "Mouse and I sneaked inside once and had a good sniff around before the humans chased us out. Humans use it to store old stuff they don't use anymore, but like to stare at."

It didn't make sense to Pierre, but then, most of what humans did was senseless to him.

Behind the museum was a graveyard for things on wheels. Warning him to be careful of broken glass, the terrier led him past the rusty skeletons of ancient cars, trucks, tractors, and other wheeled contraptions Pierre had sometimes seen rolling through fields along the highway. There was even a kind of car made of wood, soft and gray with age. It had no engine, but there was a wooden shaft at the front where Pierre supposed humans could hook themselves up and pull.

A flash of lightning lit up an old combine. Dare pushed through a ragged curtain of weeds under the rusty blades—and vanished. Pierre jumped back and snorted in surprise.

Dare popped back into sight. "What are you waiting for? Come on!"

"Where did you go?"

"Follow me, and you'll see."

Dare ducked back through the weeds. Pierre trotted after her, and fell headfirst into a hole in the ground. Mew slipped out of his mouth and went tumbling down a dark tunnel.

"This is a rabbit's burrow!" he cried, digging his claws into the dirt that surrounded him. He could neither back up nor turn around. He scrambled forward and found himself in an underground chamber. As his eyes adjusted to the darkness he saw Dare lounging on a nest of stuffing probably torn from the seat of one of the old cars. Mew sat in the middle of the floor, blinking sleepily at her new surroundings. She yawned, curled up beside Dare, and went back to sleep.

"A badger's sett," Dare corrected as Pierre frantically sniffed and pawed at the walls, trying to overcome his claustrophobia. "It used to be a rabbit warren, until a pair of badgers took it over. The badgers moved out when the humans dragged all those cars and things into this field. Mouse and I made it our den."

"Dogs don't live in burrows!" He hated closed-in

spaces. One of the reasons he did so well at agility trials was that he broke all the speed records in his hurry to get through the tunnel section.

"Why not? It's warm in the winter, cool in the summer. Come on out, Mouse. It's safe. I've already had my shake."

A whiskered snout poked out of a small side tunnel. After a cautious sniff, the rest of Mouse squirmed into sight. He flinched and growled as Dare jumped up and shook herself, flinging mud all over the burrow. "Why do you always do that?" he snapped.

Pierre relaxed enough to sit down. "How do you know the Bull Dogs are looking for me?"

"After you left we ran into one of his pack," Mouse said. "Ratter told us Bull was mad enough to take a bite out of the sidewalk, and he was looking for the poodle who'd made a fool of him."

"I wouldn't want to be in your paws, Curly," Dare said.

"I'm sure my humans will return before I run into the Bull Dogs again," Pierre said. "As for tonight—are you sure this place is safe?"

"Ratter is the only Bull Dog small enough to follow us in here, and we can handle him. There's even a secret escape tunnel."

"Dare, if Bull knows we're helping him, he might make even more trouble for us," Mouse whispered.

"Oh, come on, Mouse. Didn't the poodle save our tails from the Bull Dogs?"

Pierre curled up beside her, humbled by the sharp nip his conscience gave him for his earlier thoughts about mongrel dogs. He breathed in the wild, wet scent of the stormy night and listened to the rain patter on the combine above the burrow. He felt safe for the first time all day. The question was, could he stay that way until his humans returned?

4
Breakfast For Three

WHEN PIERRE AWOKE in the morning, Dare was gone. This didn't worry him. Mew was gone too. This did worry him. He climbed up to the tunnel entrance and had a quick look around. Finding no sign of her, he ducked back down into the burrow.

"Mew?" Was she lost in the network of tunnels? "Mew! *Mew*!"

Mouse lifted his head irritably. "Wake up, poodle. You're having a cat nightmare."

"I'm calling the pup. She's disappeared. You search these smaller tunnels while I check out the escape tunnel."

Pierre surfaced in a patch of thistles with spiky round purple blossoms. In front of him, miles of silky prairie grass rippled in the breeze. The cheerful tune of a distant meadowlark greeted the morning.

The only creature in sight was a sleepy owl perched on the edge of a rusty can, an owl no larger than a human's hand. When Pierre popped out of his burrow, the owl darted into its own hole in the ground. A crowd of tiny feathered faces filled the opening of the burrow, staring at Pierre with eyes like golden marbles. Rodents, dogs, birds—everything lived underground in this strange land.

"I wouldn't be surprised to see humans crawl into burrows at the end of the day," he said.

"They do." Mouse emerged from the escape tunnel with a yawn and a stretch. "Why do you think they dig a big hole before they build a house? Did you find the pup?"

"No. Do you think Dare took her somewhere?"

"No—Dare left before sunrise, alone. She wanted to collect a few scents before breakfast."

Pierre glanced back toward the museum and gave a relieved sigh as Mew burst out of a patch of dandelions under the wooden car. "There she is. She found a family of kittens to play with."

Mouse choked on a yawn. "Kittens? Where?"

"There—see, she's chasing three black and white kittens around those big wheels—"

Mouse gave a yelp that sent Pierre's ears straight up. "Those aren't kittens!"

The Chihuahua yapped frantically until Mew scampered over to them. The animals that weren't kittens scurried under an old red tractor.

"You scared my new friends," Mew complained.

Mouse shuddered. "Trust me, little one, skunks are no one's friends."

Mew sighed. "I miss the farm. I'd be getting slops and fresh milk for breakfast now. Let's find a garden and pretend we're rabbits again."

A fat beetle crawled across Mouse's foot. He snapped it up and crunched noisily. "Salad for breakfast? Ugh. I'll take you to a restaurant."

"We tried one of those places already," Pierre said. "It didn't work. They threw us out."

Mouse's whiskers quivered in horror. "You went *inside?* Oh no no no, that's not the way to do it! Come on, I'll show you."

He took them to the only street in town with traffic lights. In an alley behind a row of shops he went up to a door seething with wonderful aromas. *Of course!* Pierre thought. They had entered through the wrong door yesterday. If they went in the back way, the humans who did the cooking would feed them. He sat down and waited to see how Mouse would get the cooks' attention. His tail wagged a fan in the dirt as he imagined heaping plates of hot food.

Instead, the Chihuahua trotted over to the garbage bin. He scrambled to the top of a stack of boxes piled against the bin and hopped right into it. Bits of trash flew over the edge. A blob of cold mashed potatoes splattered Pierre's paws. He leaped back in horror.

"Garbage?" he yelped. "You expect us to eat garbage?"

Mouse's head popped over the edge of the bin. "Is that enough, or do you want more?" Receiving no reply, he jumped to the ground among the smelly mess his digging paws had propelled out of the garbage bin. Gulping down some fatty roast beef, he advised, "Eat fast. You won't have long."

He was right. Pierre had barely sampled his scattered breakfast when the cafe's back door banged open and a woman in an apron ran at them, yelling and flapping her arms. Mouse scurried away, but Pierre and Mew just stared in astonishment at this bizarre behavior. The woman hurled an empty jar. It shattered against the garbage bin just above their heads. The two dogs ran. They joined Mouse under the wooden doorstep of a little cheese shop.

"That woman called us—" Pierre could barely bring himself to say it— "Bad Dogs." He, Prince Pierrot, a Bad Dog? It was unthinkable.

"You'll get used to it." Mouse licked his whiskers. "Still hungry?"

"Not hungry enough to go through that again. Take us back to the service station."

At the Gas 'n' Go a motor home idled in the parking lot. Pierre dashed toward it, but then saw the tangled clump of bicycles hanging from the back bumper. It wasn't his.

"I used to do that all the time, after my humans abandoned me," Mouse said. "I chased every red car in town. I ran to every man with a beard and every woman with brown hair, but it was never their car, and it was never them."

"My humans haven't abandoned me." Pierre didn't like how desperate he sounded. He said more firmly,

"They must not have noticed I was missing until they stopped for the night. It's just a matter of time before they remember this place and come back to look."

"Are you going to wait, then?" Mouse asked.

Pierre glanced at Mew. It wasn't fair to make her sit with him in this hot parking lot. What if the Bull Dogs came back? What if his humans showed up, but didn't want to take the lost pup with them? Maybe Dare and Mouse could take care of her. They would teach her to be a stray, to eat garbage and steal from humans to survive.

"No, Mouse, not just yet," Pierre said. "I'm going to take Mew back to her farm, like I should have done yesterday."

Mew yipped and did a wiggly little dance. Mouse's eyes opened wide. "A farm? You're going into the country?"

Pierre picked up Mew and loped toward the highway. "If my humans don't return today, I'll see you back at the burrow tonight. If they do—good-bye, and thanks for everything!"

"Wait, it's too dangerous! There's a—"

Mouse's yaps were drowned out by the roar of a passing semi-trailer (or galloping tractor, as Mew called it). By the time it was gone, Pierre and Mew were far down the highway. Mouse didn't follow.

5

Where Green Chickens and Buffalo Roam

PIERRE BROUGHT MEW to the old poplar tree beside the highway. The poor cat was gone from the ditch. Perhaps her humans had found her and had taken her away to do whatever humans do with animals whose souls have gone to the Forever Field.

"Which way was your mother taking you, Mew?" Pierre asked.

"That way, across the wheat field." She pointed her nose across a field of tall green grass. Pierre could see two farms in that direction. Aiming for the nearest one, he crossed the highway and carried her into the field. The dampness from last night's storm soaked quickly through his fur, but he was relieved to get away from the open road. He really had to get over this fear that without buildings or trees to hold it up, the great blue sky would collapse and crush him.

Mew wiggled and pedaled her paws as Pierre pushed through the emerald stalks that stretched above his head. "They tickle!"

"Don't the humans around here know about lawn mowers?" Pierre dropped her and sprang into the air to make sure he was going in the right direction. He felt like a flea hopping across the back of a giant green dog. When he moved on, he nearly stumbled into a nest of small, speckled eggs hidden beneath the sweet-smelling shrubs that grew around a tall stone. As he and Mew sniffed the nest, a brown bird with a pair of black bands around its white throat limped past them, dragging one wing on the ground and chirping piteously.

"That's a killdeer, and she's faking," Mew said, but they followed her anyhow. Once they were far from her nest she lifted the injured wing and sailed into the sky, shrieking with laughter. Her flight startled a jackrabbit hidden in the grass. It flashed past the dogs and bounded away, its powerful back legs carrying it high over the wheat with every leap. Mew scrambled after it, yipping.

"It's five times bigger than you," Pierre called after her. "What will you do with it?"

Intent on the capture of the mighty jackrabbit, Mew ignored him. Oh, well. He could always track her down if she got lost. He reached the edge of the field and stepped into the open.

To his left was a tall yellow house, to his right a red barn with a fence around it to contain a small herd of shaggy brown animals with short curved horns. The animals were separated into two corrals that opened into a wide pasture on the other side of the farm. Near the barn stood three buildings that looked like huge metal trashcans with pointed lids. A wire fence enclosed a small white shed. Within the enclosure half a dozen birds squatted sleepily in patches of sunlight flickering through a stand of evergreens.

Pierre had learned a little about farms from a champion border collie who specialized in herding sheep. He didn't see any sheep, but those woolly brown things with the horns must be cows of some sort. They were odd-looking beasts. Their heavy round heads hung low from tall, shaggy shoulders, which sloped down to skinny hindquarters. Add a bit of curl to the coat, a pom-pom tail and long ears instead of horns, and you'd have a poodle with the French cut. A very *large* poodle. Pierre looked at their powerful chests and thick legs, and wondered how the humans ever managed to milk them. Their udders seemed to be missing.

Mew caught up to him, panting and rabbitless. Her ears drooped. "This isn't my farm."

Pierre gave the top of her head a comforting lick. "Let's have a look anyhow. I've never been to a farm."

A calf put her head through the wooden fence surrounding the barn to get a closer look at them. Pierre stood on his hind legs and touched her large damp nose with his. He was about to speak when she snorted all over him. He fell over backwards, sputtering in disgust.

"Don't go in there," Mew warned. "Especially don't go near the bulls. They'll toss you to the moon if they catch you. Besides, if you step in that brown stuff you'll smell even worse."

"What do you mean, 'worse'?"

"Well, you *are* a dog."

Pierre shook the slime from his fur and eyed the birds within the wire fence. Their bright blue-and-green feathers glittered like the paint of a new car. Their wings were blue, and their tail feathers, which swept out behind them like a trailing skirt, were tipped with egg-shaped spots of green, blue and bronze. At the sight of the dogs one of the birds raised its long tail and spread it into a beautiful rainbow fan.

"There's no roof on that fence," Pierre said. "Why don't these chickens fly away?"

Mew stared at him, then laughed so hard she rolled on the ground with her paws in the air. "Those aren't chickens! Chickens are white or brown with short tails."

"These are obviously chickens from the city," Pierre said stiffly. "Naturally they'd wear fancier feathers than your boring country chickens." He took another look at the birds. It must be those heavy tails that kept them from flying. He experienced a sudden urge to be a Bad Dog. "Maybe we could chase them."

"Oh, no!" Mew's puppy-blue eyes widened in shock. "You mustn't chase anything that belongs to the farm. That's the big rule."

"Not even just a little?"

"No," Mew said firmly.

"Then let's keep looking for your farm. Maybe that dog knows where it is."

A large dog had appeared from behind the barn,

a gray husky with a white face and yellow eyes. He moved the way Dare had sneaked up on Titan: slowly, with his head low to the ground. He ignored the other two dogs. His attention was on the green chickens.

"He doesn't look like a farm dog," Mew said.

The big cows snorted and pawed the ground as the dog crept up to the fence. He slipped between the rough wooden poles, dropped down onto one of the brown piles Mew had warned Pierre about, and rolled in it.

"Ew!" Mew wrinkled her nose. "What's he doing that for?"

"He must be a scent collector, like Dare."

The strange dog rolled to his feet and slipped back under the fence. Instead of coming toward Pierre and Mew, he moved away behind the white shed. A long minute passed.

Suddenly the husky ran out from behind the shed and leaped at the tall wire fence, which collapsed under his weight. He grabbed one of the birds by the neck and shook it fiercely, then dropped it to the ground, where it fluttered weakly. The others fled into the white shed, flapping and shrieking. One, a brown-and-green hen, simply fainted. The husky licked his lips and picked it up.

"Hey!" Mew yipped. "Never bite the farm animals! Bad dog! Bad dog!"

Mew scrambled over the broken fence and charged at the husky. The husky ignored her. He was trying to work out a way to pick up both birds at once. Mew sank her sharp milk teeth into his foot. His muffled yelp woke the hen in his jaws. She squawked and flapped her wings in his face until he was forced to drop her. The hysterical bird trampled Mew in her haste to get away. The stunned pup lay between the husky's front paws, a scrap of dusty fur so tiny it took the husky a few moments to find her.

In those few moments, Pierre jumped the broken fence, snatched Mew out from under the husky's nose and ran toward the barn. The big dog followed, snarling, but the wooden fence slowed him down for a moment. By the time he scrambled between the heavy poles Pierre was among the herd, dodging through a forest of thick legs. It was like doing the weave poles, except these poles tried to kick his head off and stomp him flat. The new mothers weren't happy at having this strange little dog scampering around their calves.

Pierre found himself trapped against a stack of hay bales piled against the barn. The cows, frightened by the husky's approach, stampeded toward him. He scrambled to the top of the bales to avoid being trampled. The husky stalked around the edge of the herd, snarling and snapping at their heels to drive them away from the barn so he could reach the haystack. The bulls roared in anger. The largest of them, obviously the herd leader, lunged against the fence that separated him from the cows and calves. The heavy poles creaked, but the fence didn't break.

The husky sprang to the top of the haystack in one leap. Pierre jumped as well, a wild, desperate leap right onto the back of the nearest cow. The herd was packed so tightly he managed to hop from back to back until he stood on the shoulders of a tall cow on the far edge of the herd.

"Try to follow us here!" he jeered at the husky, but his words were drowned out by a terrible roar from the cow beneath him. It wasn't a cow at all— it was the head bull. Pierre had jumped over the fence without noticing.

The bull turned away from the fence and thundered around the corral, bellowing in rage. Terrified, Pierre dropped Mew between his front paws and gripped the bull's woolly mane in his teeth. The bull caught sight of the husky standing on top of the haystack, and charged the fence. Pierre gulped and closed his eyes. There was a terrible crack as the poles split in half, followed by a thump as the bull struck the haystack. Suddenly the husky lay across the bull's horns, eye-to-eye with Pierre. The bull galloped across the corral and gave his head a mighty toss. The dogs sailed over the fence and landed in a heap near the chicken shed, fortunately with the husky on the bottom.

A door slammed at the house. The husky shook Pierre and Mew off, grabbed the dead bird, and loped away across the fields. Pierre staggered to his feet and nosed Mew anxiously.

"Are you all right, Mew?"

"There's a feather in my ear and wool in my teeth, but otherwise I'm all right. What a ride!"

Pierre pawed at the handful of beautiful green

feathers the husky had left behind. "Well, there's one bird that's gone to the Forever Field," he said, trying not to sound as shaken as he felt. He had never seen anything killed before. "Or maybe for chickens it's the Forever Farm."

"That dog's going to get himself shot." Mew didn't seem as sad about the slaughtered bird as he thought she'd be. "He's a killer dog."

"Shot?" Pierre asked. "You mean, like when the vet pokes a needle into your rump?"

A rumpled, sleepy human trotted toward them from the house. In his hand was a small radio, identical to the one attached to one of the walls of the white shed. He looked at the ruined wire fence, at the blood and feathers on the ground, and at the two dogs. He said some angry words and ran back to the house. Pierre sat down and waited for him to return. Maybe, to reward them for scaring away the husky, he was going to feed them.

When the man returned he had something in his hands, but it wasn't food. Pierre had seen humans use this thing at a field trial his humans had attended once. A hunting dog would find a bird hidden in tall grass or bushes and freeze into a pointing position until his human allowed him to scare it into flight. The human would aim this stick and with a loud bang make the bird fall out of the sky so the dog could bring it back to him.

The hunting dogs called it a gun. Pierre had never seen a gun pointed at a dog—until now.

"Look out!" Mew cried.

There was a loud crack and the dirt between Pierre's front paws exploded in his face. He leaped into the air. A second shot singed his ear. He snatched up Mew and raced toward the wheat field. The gun went off a third time, and something bit his leg. He yelped and fell, rolling across the ground. Mew cried in terror. He scrambled to his feet and limped into the field, hiding himself and Mew among the wheat. The gun cracked again, the bullet tearing through the green stalks above Pierre's head.

Pierre ran until he reached the highway. He dropped Mew and looked at his hind leg. A bullet had nicked it just above the paw. It was bleeding.

"Why did he shoot at us?" Mew cried. "Oh, I know why. He thinks we killed the bird. He thinks we're killer dogs! We'll never be safe now!"

"You'll be safe on your farm—if I can ever find it." Pierre licked his wound, feeling like a failure. He had lost the competition, he had lost his humans, and he had nearly lost his life. He couldn't even find a stupid farm on the open prairie. "Maybe Dare and Mouse will help us look for it."

Mew sighed. "It will be lonely there without my brothers and sisters."

"Did your humans give them away?"

"No. Snowball got stepped on by a cow. Ginger got run over by the tractor. Toby got eaten by a fox. Smoky climbed into the engine of the farmer's truck to get warm, and when the farmer started the motor—"

"You mean they all *died*? Mew, that's terrible! Why didn't you tell me farms are so dangerous? There's no way I'm taking you back there!"

"That's okay. I'd rather stay with you and Dare and Mouse, anyway. Even if you are dogs."

"Listen, Mew, there's something you have to know." Pierre took a deep breath. "You are not a kitten. You're a pup."

"You shut up! My mother was a cat, my brothers and sister were cats, and so am I!"

Pierre jumped back as Mew tried to scratch his nose. "But Mew, didn't you notice your ears were longer than theirs?"

"Mother said it was because the geese tugged on them when I was smaller."

"And your tail is shorter."

"Mother said it was because the rats chewed it in half." She wrinkled her forehead thoughtfully. "But you know, I was the only one who made the weird sound—yip!—that Mother never liked."

"That's a dog sound. It's called a bark."

"You mean I'll grow up to be a dog, just like you?" Mew cringed in horror.

"Not exactly like me, but you'll probably end up the same size, because it looks like you have a lot of beagle in you."

Mew padded over to a puddle of rainwater in the ditch and stared down at her reflection. "But I don't want to be a dog," she said finally.

"Of course you do! Dogs are far superior to cats."

"Why?"

"Because we..." Pierre hesitated. "Well, just because."

"But I don't know anything about being a dog."

"Just use me as your role model, and you'll do fine."

Mew politely said nothing.

6
A Day in the Life
of a Prairie Dog

DARE AND MOUSE were waiting for them at the Gas 'n' Go.

"You're alive!" Dare observed, sniffing him thoroughly from nose to tail. "And you've picked up an impressive collection of scents. Garbage bin mold, sage, wheat, manure, hay, feathers—and, if I'm not mistaken, blood. Mouse should have warned you how dangerous it is out there. Badgers, foxes, coyotes—there are all kinds of animals who could give dogs our size a lot of trouble. You could have run into that wild dog, Wolf, or got shot at by a farmer."

61

"We did see a vicious husky," Pierre said.

"I bit him!" Mew added.

"And we did get shot at by a farmer."

"He shot Pierre!"

"These two find more trouble in a day than we do in a year," Mouse said to Dare as Pierre showed off the bullet wound on his leg.

Dare gave Pierre's leg a worried sniff. "We'd better do something about that. Follow me."

She took them to Silvertree Park, a hilly stretch of soft grass bordered by rows of trees and beds of flowers. Humans walked slowly along the paved paths, or ran as if they had a long, long way to go. On a block of stone in the center of the park stood a bronze statue of a man in a uniform. Pierre took an instant dislike to it. The man held a gun.

Dare led the others to one of the iron benches beside a creek that flowed under a wooden bridge. A white-haired man was tossing bits of bread into the water for a pair of Canada geese and their goslings. At his feet sat the droopiest basset hound Pierre had ever seen. His ears dragged on the ground, his hide hung in heavy folds, his belly nearly scraped the ground. Even his eyes drooped, giving him an expression sad enough to bring tears to Pierre's own eyes.

"Good morning, Dare, Mouse." The hound's slow, deep voice turned the greeting into a tragedy. "Who are your friends?"

"Pierre and Mew," Dare said.

"They've lost their humans, Old Sam," Mouse explained.

Old Sam looked even more mournful. "I'm sorry to hear that. Now pup, that's not wise," he added as Mew crept toward the water's edge, where a piece of bread had fallen short. One of the geese swept toward her, flapping its wide wings and hissing like a cat. Mew hissed back, much to the goose's surprise. Mew snatched up the bread and ran, but not quickly enough. The goose stretched out its long neck and gave the pup's tail a fierce snap. Mew yipped and ducked behind Pierre.

The old man laughed and leaned over the dogs. "Well, if it isn't our little Daredevil and her side-kick Mouse. I see you've brought guests. How do you do?" He held out a hand and Pierre politely put his paw into it. Mew licked it, then tried to nibble on his gnarled knuckles.

"It's rude to chew on humans, Mew," Pierre said.

"What happened to your poor leg?" The man took out a clean hanky and cut a strip from it with his pocket knife. He wrapped it around Pierre's injured leg, his gentle voice soothing the pain away. This was a new experience for Pierre—a human speaking to him without scolding, praising or giving commands.

"I like your human, Old Sam," Pierre said as Mr. Abram gave him a final pat on the head and went back to feeding the geese.

"Mouse and I like him too," Dare said. "He gave us our names."

"He's nice," Mew said. "He isn't shouting, chasing or shooting us."

"Good heavens, I should hope not!" Old Sam exclaimed. "Dare, have you been getting your new friends into trouble?"

"I'm the one trying to keep them *out* of trouble!"

"Then I hope you warned them to avoid the Bull Dogs, and advised them not to go into the country."

Dare just sighed.

"Was that husky we saw the wild dog you were talking about?" Pierre asked her.

"Sounds like it. Wolf showed up earlier this

spring. They say he's part wolf and was born wild in the forests up north. He roams the countryside, killing small animals like rabbits and chickens for food."

"How very unsporting, to hunt barnyard fowl," Old Sam said.

"Old Sam was a hunting dog in a country away across the sea," Dare told Pierre and Mew.

"Mr. Abram and I shared some wonderful adventures when we were younger," Old Sam agreed. "But he retired me at a young age. I couldn't bear to see the poor foxes or rabbits killed. I led the rest of the pack astray so our prey could escape. Rather embarrassing for poor Mr. Abram."

"Old Sam is very wise," Mouse said. "You can ask him anything."

"Why is Pierre's fur cut in such a sissy way?" Mew asked.

"Long ago poodles were used as hunting dogs," Old Sam explained. "They were especially good at retrieving birds from the water. Their coats were trimmed to leave thick puffs of fur on their chests and leg joints to protect them from the cold water."

Pierre thrust his chest out proudly. No wonder he loved to chase birds. It was in his blood.

"A hunting poodle!" Dare scoffed. "He couldn't catch anything bigger than a flea."

"Appearances can be deceiving. Poodles are quick, courageous and intelligent. When Mr. Abram and I visited France, many of the stray dog packs there were led by poodles."

Pierre was feeling more dangerous by the moment.

"Why must I turn around three times before I lie down?" he asked.

"For luck."

"Why do we howl at the moon?" Dare asked.

"Because it is there."

"When you greet a human, should you sniff his tail from the front or the back?" Mouse asked.

"I wouldn't worry about it, Mouse. Either way, you aren't tall enough. Whatever is that youngster doing?" Old Sam cocked his head at Mew. The pup crouched in the grass, hindquarters wriggling.

"I'm playing Catch-a-Mouse." She pounced on a rustling leaf. "One day I'll be good enough to catch a real mouse. Haven't you ever played it, Old Sam?"

"I'm afraid not. I've never really developed a taste for mice."

"Only cats chase mice," Pierre reminded the pup.

"Then what do dogs chase?"

"Cats," Dare said.

"Speaking of which, there's that audacious creature who had the nerve to mark Mr. Abram," Old Sam said in an offended tone.

A sleek orange cat prowled through the playground in the middle of the park, brushing her furry cheek against the legs of the small children who played there. Those poor little humans had no idea they had just become her property. The cat was using the scent glands in her cheeks to mark her ownership of anything that caught her fancy.

"Eight, nine," the cat purred, scraping her cheek against a young woman holding a baby. "Nine new humans for my collection."

"I encourage you to remove that despicable feline from our immediate vicinity," Old Sam said.

Dare cocked her head. "What?"

"Chase that cat!" Old Sam translated.

Dare tore across the park, barking madly. "Keep your greedy face off Mr. Abram! He's ours!"

"Why don't you pee on him, then?" the cat suggested snidely. "Isn't that how you dogs mark your property?"

"Snobby toe-licker!" Dare howled.

"Smelly rump-sniffer!" the cat screamed.

They clashed in a noisy whirlwind of teeth, claws and flying fur. Moments later the cat crouched on a tree branch, hissing and spitting, and Dare had a few new claw marks to add to her scars.

Mr. Abram shook his head and clicked his tongue at Dare as she limped back to the creek. "It serves you right," Mew said.

"Oh, come on, pup. If you ever want to be a real dog you have to learn to hate cats. That's a rule."

"Then I don't want to be a dog anymore."

Dare licked her scratched nose. "Cats are mean. They're stupid. They sit there and stare at you with that snooty look on their faces, and you just *know* they're thinking they're so much better than—"

"My mother wasn't like that," Mew said. "She took good care of me, even though I was a pup and not a kitten. She was the best mother in the world."

Dare laid her ears back in remorse. "Aw, I'm sorry, pup. Don't cry. Hey, Mouse doesn't chase cats either. They chase him." Mew laughed, but Mouse didn't look very amused.

"Good heavens, how late it is getting. I must take Mr. Abram home for his morning nap." Old Sam laid his droopy muzzle across the old gentleman's knee and gazed sorrowfully at him. Mr. Abram rubbed the hound's long ears, then hoisted himself up with his cane and let Old Sam lead him out of the park. Pierre stared after them and sighed.

"I suppose I should get back to the service station to wait for my own humans," he said.

"Later," Dare said. "It's time for me to play outfield."

"Play what?"

"I'll show you."

Dare took them to the main doors of a large building that turned out to be a kennel for human pups. A blaring bell signaled their release into the fenced yard for exercise. Pierre cringed against the brick wall as the children noticed the dogs. It was like being surrounded by hundreds of giant yappy Pomeranians. Mew was so frightened, she tried to hide under Mouse.

When a large group of children ran by, each wearing a large leather glove on one hand, Dare followed them. The children spread out across the field behind their kennel. Dare watched them throw a ball back and forth until one of them hit it with a heavy wooden stick. As the ball rolled past her, Dare raced after it and brought it back to one of the children, who threw it to another team-mate. It looked like so much fun, Pierre joined her, hopping around as best he could on three legs. The children cheered every time one of the dogs caught the ball. They even cheered when Dare, overcome by her thieving instincts, ran away with the ball and tried to bury it in the outfield.

The bell rang again and the children trudged reluctantly back into their kennel. Pierre was sorry to see them go. Who would have thought humans could be so much fun?

Mouse suddenly cocked his head, swiveling his large ears like a bat listening for moths. "Plane, Dare!"

The dogs looked up and saw a small airplane descending on Silvertree.

"Come on!" Dare grabbed Mew and ran after it. Pierre hung back.

"But I have to get back to the—"

"Hurry! There's not much time!"

Pierre gave up and followed her.

The plane was just coming in for a landing at the small airstrip outside of town. Dare ran straight onto the runway, barking, and scattered a flock of ducks that must have wandered over from the nearby creek.

"If we don't clear the runway, they might fly up and smack into the plane!" Dare panted as she ran past Pierre, trying to shoo a stubborn duck off the tarmac. "It could crash!"

At last, birds he was allowed to chase! Pierre ran around madly, barking at the top of his lungs until the entire flock had flown away. The dogs scrambled off the runway just as the plane touched down. It rolled to a stop and several humans climbed out, waving at the dogs.

Dare trotted over to the small building at the edge of the landing strip. A woman came outside to meet her.

"Good work, girl! Those brainless ducks would be feather pillows if not for you. Here's your wages, and some for your new assistant, too." She handed them some dog biscuits. She had some for Mew and Mouse as well, although they had only barked encouragement from the sidelines.

"See you next time!" she called as the dogs headed back to town.

"It's hard work being a stray," Pierre observed.

"We can't all perform tricks for a living, like some dogs," Dare said.

This reminded Pierre of his own humans. "I really have to get back to the service station now."

"It's lunchtime. The Bull Dogs will be there, sniffing around the back alley for leftovers. Better wait till later."

The dogs went back to the park and took a long nap under the wooden bridge. When they awoke they chased each other across the grass and played hide-and-seek among the trees and flower beds. Mew almost managed to climb a tree while chasing a squirrel. She fell off and tumbled into the creek when Pierre reminded her dogs couldn't climb trees. He had to jump in and rescue her. Pups, he was discovering, needed a lot of rescuing.

Dare led them back to Titan's house to witness another daring raid on the Great Dane's supper. From there they snuck into a garden and liberated a few carrots and peas. They were daring each other to take a bite of the hot, spicy radishes when Dare tensed, sniffing the air.

"Down!" she growled softly. They crouched in the holes they had dug as Bull and his Bull Dogs sauntered down the alley behind the garden. Bull stopped and sniffed suspiciously in their direction. He couldn't see anything through the thick carrot tops, so he moved on. The dogs scrambled out of the garden and didn't stop until they reached their burrow.

"Being a stray isn't so bad, is it?" Dare said as they settled into the soft nest of their underground den.

"As long as we stay out of Bull's way." Pierre shook a spider squeamishly off his paw. Mouse scooped it up with his tongue and swallowed it. One leg got caught in his teeth and stayed there, wriggling. Pierre shuddered and turned to Dare. "How long have you been a stray, Dare?"

"Since I was a pup. I was born in the old grain elevator across the highway. My mother keeps the rats away for the humans who work there. My brother and I thought living in town would be more exciting than chasing rodents, so we came here when we were big enough to cross the highway."

"Where's your brother now?"

"Ratter joined the Bull Dogs. Me, I don't like packs."

"Aren't we a pack?" Mew asked.

Dare looked startled. "I guess we are."

"Then we should have a name."

"The Prairie Dogs," Pierre joked, thinking back to that small burrowing animal on the highway.

"I want to be a stray forever." Mew snuggled comfortably between Pierre and Dare. Pierre winced as he saw a pair of fleas hop from her back onto his.

"You know, there are some things about being a stray we haven't told you," Mouse spoke up. "Like how in the winter it's so cold your ears and tail can freeze right off."

"Your ears are too long anyway," Dare said, "and there's not enough left of your tail to freeze off."

"It's so cold all the water freezes and you have to eat snow," Mouse continued. "Humans don't go outside much, so you never get enough food. Also, when you're sick or hurt there's no one to take care of you. And strays get sick a lot."

"My humans will be back long before any of that happens," Pierre assured him. "And the three of you are welcome to come home with me. I'm sure I could convince them to take you in."

Dare snorted, and Mouse blinked sadly at him. Their disbelief reminded Pierre that an entire day had passed since his humans had driven away, and they still hadn't returned for him.

What if they *didn't* return for him?

As he drifted off to sleep, Pierre realized the thought of his humans never coming back didn't bother him as much today as it had yesterday.

7
The Bull Dogs

DAYS SLIPPED AWAY, and Pierre's visits to the Gas 'n' Go grew shorter and fewer. His adventures with Dare, Mouse and Mew kept him so busy, he often forgot he had humans who might be looking for him.

One morning the dogs woke long after sunrise (they had stayed up late to howl at the moon and so were sleeping in) and took a run across the fields. A puppyish mood grabbed them. They chased gophers and butterflies. They barked at the sun. They rolled around in the silky foxtails, nipping one another's ears and tails and growling ferociously.

Mouse discovered a bumblebee bumping around a patch of prairie lilies. His eyes widened and his ears quivered as he watched it crawl into one of the spotted orange blossoms.

"Don't do it, Mouse," Dare warned. "You know what will happen."

Mouse licked his muzzle. "But it looks so… *juicy*. I bet I could catch just one without getting stung."

"Sure, it always *starts* with 'just one', and the next thing you know you're going after the whole hive! Just say 'no', Mouse."

"Look," Pierre said. Their wild romp had carried them to a square of short green grass surrounded by a low hedge. A man walked among rows of carved white and gray stones within the hedge. A basset hound trotted at the man's heels, his low-slung belly nearly dragging on the ground.

"It's Old Sam and Mr. Abram," Pierre said. "Let's say hello."

Dare shuddered. "I don't like the graveyard. We'll see them later at the park. Come on, let's go for breakfast."

"Go ahead. I'll catch up to you." Pierre was no longer afraid of losing his way in Silvertree. "And don't let Mew sneak away and play with those stinking skunks again!"

As the others ran back toward town, he wiggled through the hedge and caught up to the pair.

"Hello, Old Sam. Beautiful morning, isn't it?"

"Indeed it is, Pierre." Old Sam's glum tone made a beautiful morning seem like the end of the world.

Mr. Abram planted his cane in the grass and lowered himself to one knee beneath an old elm tree. He placed a bouquet of red roses at the base of a tall white stone. Old Sam's sadness was nothing compared to the sorrow Pierre sensed from the human.

"She wishes he wouldn't grieve so," Old Sam said.

"Who wishes?"

Old Sam closed his eyes. "Can't you feel her?"

Feel whom? Pierre shut his own eyes. The warm breeze seemed to carry the scent of lilac perfume. He felt the touch of a gentle hand on his head. When he opened his eyes, the slender figure of a woman was bending over Mr. Abram. Pierre blinked, and she was gone.

The hound ambled over and leaned his wrinkled head against Mr. Abram's knee. The old man turned and saw Pierre.

"Why, good morning, my friend!" He plucked a few stray foxtails out of the tangled curls of Pierre's ears. "I see you've escaped the company of Daredevil and Mouse. Just as well; they are sure to be a bad influence on you. Care to join us?"

Pierre followed the pair out of the cemetery and

down the narrow lane that led back into town. They passed the museum and strolled through one of the newer areas of Silvertree. Mr. Abram stopped at the edge of one of the new lots. There was no lawn, no fence—just bare dirt and the empty wooden framework of a half-built house. The old man stared up at the wooden skeleton, then sighed and turned away.

"Your human seems so sad this morning, Old Sam," Pierre said as Mr. Abram made his way to the park.

"He's lonely," the hound replied.

"There are always crowds of humans around the park. Why don't they come over and talk to him?"

"I suppose they have no use for one so old."

Pierre snorted. "Humans! They fill up a whole museum with old junk to look at, but they ignore the best antiques of all—other humans."

"I wish I knew how to ease his grief," the hound sighed.

"Let me try," Pierre said.

Pierre waited for Mr. Abram to seat himself on his favorite park bench, then sprang into action. He walked a circle on his front paws. He did backward flips. He snapped imaginary flies out of the air. He rolled onto his back and pretended to be stuck to the ground. He chased his tail until he accidentally smacked his head against a tree.

"Good heavens. You appear to have gone quite mad," Old Sam observed sadly.

Mr. Abram managed a watery smile. Encouraged, Pierre coaxed Old Sam to join him. The sight of the portly old hound trying to imitate Pierre's acrobatics was too much for Mr. Abram. He laughed until tears dribbled into his moustache. Suddenly Pierre realised the human's eyes had closed. His chin rested on his chest.

"I've killed him!" Pierre cried. "He's laughed himself to death."

"He's only asleep," Old Sam assured him, puffing from his exertions. "Thank you so much for lifting his spirits. Oh, good morning."

Dare, Mouse and Mew had arrived sometime during the performance. They kept their distance and looked at Pierre and Old Sam suspiciously. Pierre could guess what they were thinking: rabies.

"Who is your friend?" Old Sam asked, for they had a new dog with them, a pretty gold-and-silver Yorkshire terrier with a pink ribbon around her head. Mouse's tail wagged wildly every time she glanced at him.

"This is Daisy, a house dog," Dare introduced her while the other dogs performed the formal circling and sniffing. "This morning she slipped outside and ran off before her humans could catch her."

"Why did you run away?" Pierre asked. Daisy glanced at him and wrinkled her nose. Her silky clean fur, expensive velvet collar and plump tummy made Pierre suddenly aware of how dirty and matted his own coat had grown in the past two weeks. It had collected enough pungent scents to make Dare jealous, and that one pair of fleas had multiplied into an entire community.

"Thee wanted uth to thow her around town," Mouse said. Pierre looked closely at him. The

Chihuahua's tongue was swollen, as if it had been stung. Mouse ducked his head guiltily.

"Won't your humans be worried about you?" Old Sam asked.

"I'll go back eventually," Daisy said. "After I've had a little fun."

"You think being a stray is fun?" Pierre asked.

"*You* seem to enjoy it," Dare pointed out. "When was the last time you went to the gas station looking for your humans?"

Pierre didn't answer. He *had* been having fun. And yet, the tricks he had just performed for Mr. Abram reminded him that he had once been a champion, with humans who bathed and fed him and gave him a warm bed at night.

"I'd never leave my humans for good," Daisy said, ignoring Pierre. "Who would fight the Roaring Red Beast for them?"

"The Roaring Red Beast?" Mew asked.

"A wicked creature," Daisy whispered. "It lives in our hallway closet. It has a long neck like a snake and a wide mouth that sucks up everything in its path. It roars like thunder and it's as red as blood!"

Mew whimpered and pressed close against Pierre.

"When I hear its terrible snarls, I know it has escaped from the closet and I come running to find one of my humans struggling with it. I attack the beast, sinking my teeth into its long neck and shaking it like a rat! My human laughs with relief that I have come to the rescue. Finally it falls silent as if it knows it is beaten and my human and I chase it back into the closet."

"You're so brave!" Mouse exclaimed.

Dare snorted. "If you want to see a real monster, we'll introduce you to a Great Dane. You can watch me steal his supper."

"Anyone could do that," Daisy said haughtily. "I could do it. In fact, I'll do it right now. No, don't talk me out of it; my mind's made up."

"That ribbon is squeezing your brain too tight, Ditzy."

"Daisy!"

Pierre feared a scrap was about to take place, but Daisy turned away from Dare and pricked up her ears. "Oh, the Bull Dogs! How exciting. I never thought I'd have the opportunity to meet them."

Pierre whirled around to find a battle-scarred bull terrier looking down at him.

"I've been looking for you, poodle," Bull growled.

Six of his pack members slunk past him to circle the park bench where the dogs had gathered. Mr. Abram slumbered on. Old Sam pressed against the human's legs, a deep snarl rumbling in his chest. Mouse swooned gracefully at Daisy's feet.

"You leave Pierre alone or I'll bite your tail off!" Mew piped up bravely from behind the others.

"I don't want to fight you, Bull," Pierre said, although a suicidal voice in the back of his mind whispered, "I bet I could take him."

"Who said I wanted to fight? What I want, poodle, is for you to join my pack."

Pierre was so surprised he sneezed, a rather embarrassing quirk he shared with most small dogs he knew. "I thought you hated me."

"Oh, I did. One pussyfoot poodle making fools of us all—I could have chewed the caps off a fire hydrant! But I need brains like yours in my pack. Someone to help us scrounge food and outsmart our enemies—a full-time job for this bunch. Join us, you and Dare both. I'll even let the rat and the brat tag along."

"Go kiss a cat, Bull," Dare growled. "I'd rather join a pack of skunks than the Bull Dogs."

Bull sniffed the air. "Smells to me like you already have."

Pierre threw a stern look at Mew, who quickly licked her paw and rubbed it across her face.

A ragged white terrier bared his yellowed teeth at Dare. "You think you're too good for us, don't you?"

"If you were smart, Ratter, you'd leave that mangy thug and go back home to help Mother hunt rats."

"And if you were smart, Dare, you'd talk your friend into making the right decision," Bull said.

"We need time to think about it," Pierre stalled. Leading a pack had sounded exciting when Old Sam talked about poodles in France, but the reality of it made him feel cold and shivery.

"Decide now," Bull said, "or in a few moments there'll be nothing left of you but a few scraps of fur." His pack drew closer.

"All right," Pierre said. "I'll join your pack, but let the others go."

"Excuse us a moment." Dare grabbed his ear in her teeth and dragged him aside. "Are you out of your mind?" she whispered.

"If I don't go along with them, they'll hurt the rest of you. They might even hurt Mr. Abram."

"That's not the reason you want to join them. You're lying, I can smell it on you."

Pierre turned his head away. "All right, maybe I'm thinking it's not such a bad idea to hang around with the Bull Dogs. Think of it—for once, other dogs—even Titan—would be afraid of *us*."

"I don't want other dogs to be afraid of me. You just want to impress that silly little Yorkie, don't you?"

"I do not! Look, are we so different from the Bull dogs? We steal from humans and damage their stuff. Humans already treat us like criminals; what have we got to lose?"

"What about your own humans? What would they think if they came back and found you running around with that vicious pack of bullies?"

"Let them think what they want. They called me a Bad Dog because I lost one stupid competition. I'll show them a Bad Dog."

"Hurry up, poodle, we don't have all day," Bull called.

"Besides, I don't think Bull is all that bad," Pierre whispered. "Maybe I can make friends with him and soften him up a little."

Dare turned her back on him. "Wake up, Mouse. Come on, Mew. There are a few too many Bull Dogs around here for my taste."

"I want to stay with Pierre," Mew protested, but Dare picked her up and carried her away. Mouse tried to convince Daisy to come with them, but she insisted on remaining behind, wiggling with excitement at being in the presence of the infamous Bull Dogs.

"Let them go," Bull said when one of his pack would have chased after them. "I'm sure Pierre here will think up a way to get them back. Well, choose your test, poodle."

"What do you mean?"

"No dog is worthy of joining the Bull Dogs until he's gone through an initiation. Come up with a test to prove your smarts and courage, or we'll find one for you."

"I know!" Daisy burst out. "He can steal Titan's lunch."

Old Sam shot her a severe glare. "Perhaps something slightly less dangerous. He could chase a cat, or, er, swim across the creek a few times—"

"No, I like the Yorkie's idea," Bull said. "Let's move out."

They set off for the Great Dane's house. Only Old Sam remained behind. He draped his head over Mr. Abram's knees and gazed sadly after Pierre, as if he never expected to see him again.

8
Titan the Terrible

MINUTES LATER THEY CROUCHED under the honeysuckle, where they had a clear view of the sleeping Great Dane. Pierre squinted at Titan's food dish, making sure there was something there to steal.

"Every day, Dare sneaks into Titan's yard and steals a bite of his supper," he said. "You'd think he'd learn to finish it off as soon as he's fed."

"Stop stalling and get on with it," Bull said.

Pierre started forward. If Dare could do this, so could he. He just wished she was here to see it.

Suddenly, a loud, rude noise erupted from Titan's back end. His humans must feed *him* Crunchy

Nibbles, too. He awoke with a snort and exploded to his feet, barking wildly in all directions, his long fangs flashing in the sunlight. Pierre ducked down among the snapdragons. At last, with a final suspicious snarl directed at his hindquarters, Titan flopped back down on the lawn and lowered his head. His growls rumbled into snores.

Pierre gulped. That fart had blown away his courage. Trembling, he crept out of the snapdragons. Copying Dare's technique, he slunk through the shadow of the bushes that lined the edge of the yard. At the apple tree he stopped. He was within range of Titan's rope. Taking a deep breath, he padded toward the sleeping giant. He froze when Daisy let out an excited yip. The others shushed her. The Great Dane never stirred. Pierre crawled the rest of the way to the huge bowl. Today it contained a hefty, juicy ham bone. It took Pierre three tries to get his jaws around it and haul it out of the bowl. He backed away and turned around, only to bump into a very large nose, a nose with a pair of wide-open eyes above it.

"Pierre's going to die! Pierre's going to die!" the Bull Dogs chanted.

Pierre ducked under Titan's chin and streaked across the yard in a blur of pumping legs and flapping ears. He stopped when he passed the apple tree, safely out of rope range. He was still alive!

And he hadn't even dropped the heavy bone. He flopped down on the grass and gnawed heroically on his prize, pretending not to notice the Great Dane's approach. The Bull Dogs barked their praise of his courage. Now he understood why Dare did this every day.

A shadow fell over him. Two forelegs like tree trunks planted themselves to either side of his head. He froze and slowly rolled his eyes skyward. Titan stared straight down at him. A short piece of chewed-off rope dangled from his collar.

"Titan is loose!" Bull roared. "Run for your lives!"

The Bull Dogs blundered back through the honeysuckle, cursing and snapping at whoever got in their way. Daisy ran with them, yelping like a pup.

Pierre darted between Titan's legs. Titan spun around and galloped after him, growling thunderously. Pierre jumped with a splash onto the bird bath, but it wasn't tall enough to escape the Dane. He sprang high into the air, making one of the amazing leaps that had made him famous in the show ring. His front paws caught a low branch of the apple tree. He hooked his back legs onto the branch and scrambled over to the tree trunk. From there he climbed up to the higher branches.

Titan sat under the tree and stared up at him.

"Dogs don't climb trees," he rumbled finally.

"This one does." Pierre balanced awkwardly on a branch and tried to look as if he enjoyed being stuck in a tree.

"My humans never bring me into the house, you know. You could bark to get their attention, but since you're a stray they'd probably just turn you over to the authorities."

"I'm perfectly happy where I am. The view is splendid."

With a crackle of honeysuckle branches, Dare burst into the yard, panting.

"There you are! I've been looking everywhere for you." She froze, one paw lifted in astonishment. "What are you doing? Dogs don't climb trees."

"Get away, Dare!" Pierre barked.

Dare ran across the yard and stopped below the apple tree. Titan, sitting on the other side of the tree, rose to his feet and strolled toward her. She ignored him.

"There's a motor home at the service station, Pierre. Your motor home!"

Pierre's heart bounced against his ribs like a rubber ball. "You're not lying to get me away from the Bull Dogs, are you?"

"I swear, there's a motor home there just like the one you described. Come on! Don't worry about Titan. Just jump down on this side of the tree. His rope doesn't reach this far."

Entranced by visions of a reunion with his humans, Pierre had actually forgotten there was a Great Dane loose in the yard. The word *rope* snapped him out of his happy daydream. Titan was standing right over Dare. She blinked in surprise at the chewed-off rope that dangled in front of her nose.

"Run!" Pierre cried, but Titan slapped a huge paw down on the terrier, flattening her to the ground.

"Please let her go, Titan," Pierre pleaded. "We'll never come near your supper again, I promise. We'll—we'll do you any favor you want."

Titan thought it over. "Well, I wouldn't mind having…"

"What? Name it, and we'll steal it for you!" Dare wheezed.

"Friends," the Dane said.

"Friends?" Pierre and Dare echoed.

"Yes, friends. I sit here all day with no one to talk to. Even when my humans take me for walks, other dogs are too scared to come near. You can't imagine how lonely it gets. That's why I let you little thieves into the yard. Chasing you around is my entire social life."

"All right, we'll invite a few dogs to drop by," Pierre said. "How does tomorrow afternoon sound?"

"Right now," Titan said firmly.

Pierre imagined his humans looking for him, giving up and leaving. He looked at Dare, squashed flat under Titan's paw.

He jumped to the ground. Titan didn't try to stop him from running out of the yard. Dare called after him, but he didn't stop.

He ran down the alley to a house he and Mew had visited their first day in Silvertree. As he squeezed under the fence a collie bounded over to him, barking, "Out of my yard! Keep away from my house and my grass and my trees! Out-out-out!"

"Pardon me, but there's an emergency just down the lane. If you would follow me," Pierre began, but the collie interrupted him with her staccato barks.

"Can't leave my post. Have to guard the yard. That's my duty."

Pierre resisted the urge to run over and bite her leg. "A truly professional guard dog would guard her entire street, wouldn't she?"

The collie hesitated. "I suppose…"

"There is a dog, a *thief*, trespassing on your street right this moment."

"It's not a scruffy little red terrier, is it?" the collie growled, her hackles rising.

"It certainly is," Pierre said.

"She ate all my Crunchy Nibbles one morning when my humans took me for a walk!"

Actually, *all* the Prairie Dogs had eaten her Crunchy Nibbles. Dare just happened to be the last one out of the yard when the collie came back. Pierre thought it would be wise not to mention that. "You'd better teach her a lesson," he urged.

Snarling, the collie leaped over the fence and followed Pierre back to Titan's yard. Mouse and Mew crouched under the bushes, staring at Titan and poor Dare in horror.

"Oh, Pierre, what will we do?" Mouse whimpered as Pierre ran past him. A moment later he squealed and fell over in a faint as the ferociously barking collie crashed through the honeysuckle.

"Turn that intruder over to me," the collie ordered sternly.

"Actually, she is my...guest." Titan stared wide-eyed at the beautiful collie.

"Who are you?"

"I am Titan, the guard dog of this house."

"What a coincidence. I'm Sheba, and I'm a guard dog too."

"That is a coincidence. Perhaps we could discuss our jobs."

"I suppose I can go off duty for a few minutes. So, how many intruders have you bagged in the past month?"

"Not many," Titan admitted. "Thought I had one last week, but it turned out to be a false alarm, a delivery man who didn't know enough to use the front door. Made him cry, poor fellow."

"A mistake any dog could make," Sheba said sympathetically.

"Good practice, though…"

With Titan engrossed in conversation, Dare was able to wriggle out from under his paw. She and Pierre woke Mouse and the four of them evacuated the yard.

"Are you all right?" Pierre asked Dare.

"I'm fine. Hurry! Find your humans!"

Pierre gave her cheek a grateful lick. "Thank you for coming to tell me. "

Dare's ears flattened against her head. "I almost didn't. But you're better off with your humans than with the Bull Dogs, even if it means we'll never see you again."

"Sure you will! Follow me so my humans can take you with us. Come on!"

He ran to the end of the alley. He could see the Gas 'n' Go from here. The motor home was—yes! It was there! He could see his male human in the parking lot, drinking from a paper cup. They had come back for him! They had forgiven him! All his resentment against them vanished. He couldn't wait to get back to his old life. He would throw himself into his training, work harder than ever to please them. He would fill their shelves with trophies. They would never have a reason to call him a Bad Dog again.

He looked over his shoulder. The others hadn't moved. They stared at him for a moment, then Dare sighed and led Mouse and Mew away. Pierre cocked his head in surprise. Then he understood. They knew his humans would never take three scruffy strays into their kennel of pedigreed poodles. And even if they did, none of his friends wanted the life of a kennel dog.

Swallowing a lump in his throat, Pierre trotted toward the parking lot. They didn't know what they'd be missing. A warm bed at night...all the food a dog could eat...soft, clean fur... all that grooming and clipping...the daily hours of training...sitting in a hot, cramped cage in a noisy building until it was time to perform...his humans' cold disappointment when he failed to win...

Pierre's steps slowed. He reminded himself that his humans took good care of him. They'd made him a champion. He had the best life a dog could ask for.

They had never played with him like the Silvertree children did, or talked to him in the kindly way of Mr. Abram, but a dog didn't need that to survive, did he?

He reached the edge of the parking lot and stopped, staring at the motor home. The man had gone back inside, but it didn't move. He must be waiting for his mate to come out of the cafe.

Finally she did come out. The pump attendant who had serviced the motor home the first time it stopped here was with her.

"At first we thought we had lost him in Regina, where we stopped for the night," she was saying to him. "Then Paul remembered we had stopped here for gas. We phoned your manager but he said there are so many stray dogs in this town he couldn't keep track of them. You're sure you haven't seen a black miniature poodle around here recently?"

The young man stopped. He had seen Pierre. Pierre took a step forward, then a step back, and another step back. "No," the attendant said slowly, meeting Pierre's eyes. "There's lots of stray dogs around Silvertree, but I haven't seen any poodles."

The woman sighed. "It will be a terrible loss for Mont Royal Kennels, but we do have a number of promising young poodles who could take his place."

She opened the passenger door, then hesitated. She glanced toward the edge of the parking lot. Something had moved there.

It was only wildflowers dancing in the wind. The woman shrugged and stepped into the motor home, which rolled down the highway and disappeared over the eastern horizon.

9
The Return of The Green Chicken Man

IF PIERRE THOUGHT LIFE would be kinder to him now that he had chosen to be a stray, he was wrong.

Not that he wasn't enjoying himself. He was living a rare life for a dog. Some days he was a creature of the countryside, tough and wild, running fleet as a fox across the open prairie. Other times he was a town dog, a friend to the children and elderly humans of the park. Some nights found him on a hilltop trading howls with the distant coyotes. Other nights he slunk through shadowy alleys, stealing whatever humans were foolish enough to leave outside.

"You live between two worlds," Old Sam remarked to him one day. "I don't quite know whether to call you wild or tame."

Pierre didn't care what he was. He had friends and freedom, and that was all that really mattered.

Mew agreed with him. As the hot prairie summer wore on, her legs stretched and strengthened until she could run nearly as swiftly as the older dogs. Her eyes changed from puppy-blue to a beautiful beagle brown. Her life on the farm became a hazy memory—except for her kitten habits, which she never really outgrew.

"You're embarrassing us," Dare complained one day when they found her playing Catch-a-Mouse with a young stray cat.

"Who chases rats and mice? Your mother, that's who," Mew replied. "Who chases birds and climbs trees? Pierre, that's who. Don't tell *me* how to act like a dog."

Life was good for the Prairie Dogs, as they called themselves now, but it wasn't the Forever Field. First, there was Pierre's promise to Titan. The Great Dane was grateful Pierre had introduced him to Sheba, but the collie's visits were short. That left long, lonely hours for Titan. He wanted more friends, and he wanted them now.

The dogs of Silvertree howled with laughter when Pierre invited them to pay Titan a social call. Pierre explained the situation and begged them to reconsider, but they had no sympathy for a lonely Great Dane.

"I'm afraid," he finally told his friends, "Titan's friends will have to be us."

The other three whined all the way to Titan's house, but Pierre stood firm, though he was a little nervous himself. It wasn't that Titan was difficult to get along with; he was quite friendly. Even Mouse finally stopped fainting and sat down to chat with the dog who could have easily inhaled him with a careless yawn. They didn't even have to talk, just sit and listen as he went on and on about Sheba—how beautiful she was, how intelligent, how brave and fierce. They learned to stay away from his hindquarters, not only because of the Crunchy Nibbles, but to avoid getting knocked head over heels by his long tail, which wagged dangerously every time someone mentioned Sheba's name. Mew loved to stalk and pounce on it, no matter how many times it sent her tumbling across the lawn.

The difficulty came when they tried to leave. Titan would ask them to stay a little longer, and a little longer more, and it just wasn't easy to say no to the big dog. Sometimes they stayed with him all day—which was just as well, because the Bull Dogs hadn't given up on Pierre.

In a town the size of Silvertree it wasn't easy for one pack of dogs to avoid another, but somehow Pierre and his friends managed it. Their favorite trick was to duck into the small drainpipes that ran under the streets. They would race through the underground tunnels like true prairie dogs. One night the Bull Dogs came nosing around their burrow, but Dare led the others into the escape tunnel. They hid among the tall purple thistles until the Bull Dogs gave up.

Daisy was Bull's new girlfriend. Mouse was heartbroken.

"One of these days," he muttered darkly every time he caught sight of Bull. "One of these days…!"

Dare decided the Prairie Dogs needed daily training exercises to keep themselves alert. To sharpen their noses they took turns hiding and tracking each other by scent, or they played Dare's favorite game, "Sniff Me and Guess Where I've Been". Pierre's nose had been dulled by city life, but Silvertree had no tall buildings to trap the thick, smoky smells created by humans and their machines. In the open air he could catch a whiff of the bull terrier from several blocks away, in plenty of time to avoid him.

There came a day, though, when the air hung so hot and still, scents seemed to just melt into the pavement. That afternoon the Prairie Dogs trotted carelessly around a street corner on their way to the park and found themselves face to face with the Bull Dogs.

Mouse snarled, "You thieving wad of fleabait, how dare you steal my girl—" and then fainted. The Bull Dogs surrounded Pierre, Dare and Mew, stepping over Mouse or on him as they circled and growled.

Bull stopped in front of Pierre. "You're with the wrong pack, Bull Dog."

"No I'm not, Bull. Joining you was a mistake. It won't happen again."

"You can't abandon the Bull Dogs that easily, poodle. Once you're in, you're a member for life."

A blue van screeched to a stop beside the sidewalk where they stood. A man stepped out, holding a pole with a short piece of rope on the end, a loop that could be pulled tight around a dog's neck. The Bull Dogs fled.

Dare nipped Mouse awake and the four Prairie Dogs ran in the opposite direction.

"Don't worry, that man's after Bull," Dare said. "He bit a human in the leg once—Bull, I mean, not the man. Humans are always trying to catch him."

As they drew near the park Pierre looked over his shoulder. The man was right behind him, with his pole and rope swinging towards him. Pierre recognized him—it was the farmer with the woolly cows and green chickens. He barked a warning, then jumped to one side. Dare and Mouse jumped to the other, and Mew skidded to a stop. The man tripped over the pup and fell flat on the sidewalk, nearly crushing her. He said some words Pierre was glad he couldn't understand.

"I don't get it," Dare panted as they galloped full speed across the park, with the angry man close behind them once more. "Why would he chase us instead of Bull?"

"That's the man who shot me," Pierre gasped. "He thinks I attacked his birds."

The man was shouting and waving at the people in the park. A crowd of teenagers ran to cut off the dogs' escape, flapping their arms and making so much noise the dogs were afraid to dodge past them. They found themselves trapped against the creek, so they jumped in. It was a slow current, easy enough to paddle across. If they could make it to the other side before the farmer reached the bridge, they would have a chance to outrun him.

"I'm losing all my scents," Dare complained.

"You never had any sense to begin with," Mouse puffed.

As Pierre's nose bumped the cattails on the opposite bank, he felt a rope tighten on his short tail. He yelped, paddling furiously as the farmer's pole towed him back through the water. Dare, Mouse and Mew watched helplessly from the far bank.

Pierre heard the wild bay of a hunting dog, and a tremendous splash swamped him. His tail slipped free of the rope as he struggled back to the surface. He paddled across the creek and scrambled through the cattails to solid ground. The farmer thrashed around in the water, trying to find his footing among the slippery weeds. Old Sam sat on the bank, looking quite pleased with himself.

Mr. Abram hastened over to the creek and poked at the man with his cane, making him fall back into the water again. "Leave those dogs alone! You ought to be trying to catch those big dogs that wreak havoc all over town, instead of wasting your time on these harmless little ones."

The man spat out a snail. "I'm not a dogcatcher. I'm an exotic animal farmer. I run Calloway's Peafowl and Bison Ranch a mile out of town."

"Peafowl?" Mr. Abram repeated. "Oh, you mean peacocks."

"That poodle destroyed one very expensive bird and spooked my herd of bison so badly I can't even get near them. He even rode my prize bull."

Mr. Abram looked at him sternly. "Sir, have you been drinking?"

"It's true, I swear! I looked out my kitchen window and there was that poodle riding my bull around the corral like he was in a rodeo. Poor old Rambo's been a nervous wreck ever since. Keeps twitching and looking over his shoulder. I intend to catch that poodle before he and his pack do any more damage to my livestock. Every time I drive to town I see those dogs running around the fields and streets like they own the place. Makes me so mad I could spit."

Calloway picked up his pole and looked around, but of course the poodle, the terrier, the Chihuahua and the pup had disappeared.

"Are you sorry you aren't a Bull Dog anymore?" Dare asked that night as they nestled in the musty bedding of their underground lair.

"Of course."

"Really?" Dare looked disappointed.

"Think of all the trouble I could have led them into! They wouldn't have survived a day."

Dare and Mew laughed, but Mouse looked worried.

"Next time Bull catches us, there won't be a man to save us," he said. "What will we do?"

"We'll do what any courageous, clever dog would do. We'll run like our ears are on fire and our tails are catching," Dare said.

Mew sighed. "Why can't we all just get along?"

"Getting along is boring," Dare said.

"I could use a little boredom," Mouse muttered.

Remembering the look in Bull's eyes as he had threatened them, Pierre agreed. He had a feeling, though, that it would be a long time before the Prairie Dogs experienced any sort of boredom in Silvertree.

10
The Dogs of War

AS IF IT WASN'T ENOUGH to have the Bull Dogs after them, now the Prairie Dogs had to watch out for Calloway as well. Every time they turned around, there he was with his pole and rope and a wild gleam in his eye. Pierre and his friends were so busy avoiding him, they didn't notice how unusually quiet the Bull Dogs had become. They were often seen carrying scraps of food around, as if they were gathering stores for the winter, although it was only the middle of summer. The Prairie Dogs didn't think much of this until one morning about a week after the incident with Calloway.

Pierre couldn't believe his eyes. Nearly every garbage bin behind the restaurants of Silvertree had been ransacked. Garbage had been strewn everywhere. It was as if someone had spent the whole night deliberately making a mess. He and his friends sniffed the bins and caught a familiar scent. Bull, of course.

The humans cleaning up the mess chased the dogs away before they could grab a bite to eat. The dogs made their way to the park. When the weather had turned hot, hordes of young humans had escaped their large brick kennel with the buzzing bells. No one had caught them yet, so the park was always full of children with snacks. On most days Mr. Abram brought treats for the dogs as well. The regular visits from the dogs seemed to do him good. He no longer spent all his time sitting on a bench. Often he brought an easel to the park and painted trees, birds, squirrels, and even Old Sam and the Prairie Dogs.

Today the Prairie Dogs arrived at the park to find it under attack. Bull and eight of his pack members were snarling and snapping at the humans in the playground. Bull himself had chased a group of children to the top of the tall metal slide. He circled it, growling, dodging a few angry adults who tried to drive him away.

"They're chasing humans," Mew cried. "That's almost as bad as chasing chickens!"

Pierre ran across the grass, sprang onto Bull's back and sank his teeth into the dog's ear. Bull yelped and gave his head a violent shake, slamming Pierre to the ground. Before he could move Bull was on top of him, crushing him with his weight. Pierre closed his eyes and waited to die.

He heard Bull yip in agony, and opened his eyes. Mew had come up behind Bull and clamped her little jaws on the sensitive joint of his hind leg. Bull howled and twisted around, but he couldn't reach her. Mew grimly hung on and let Bull drag her around in yelping circles.

The Bull Dogs charged over to rescue their leader. Dare and Ratter smashed together in a snarling tangle. Mouse nipped at the legs of the Bull Dogs, then sprang onto the hot slide and scurried up its slope when they turned on him. The sheepdog and the boxer who tried to follow him ended up in a sandy heap at the bottom of the slide. Mouse crouched among the cheering children and yapped tauntingly at the dogs.

The Bull Dogs couldn't remove Mew without causing their leader more pain, so they turned their attention to Pierre. There was only one thing to do. He chased his tail. The Bull Dogs skidded to a halt and stared down at him as he spun around and around. They sat down and cocked their heads, hypnotized by this whirling furry blur.

Someone must have gone for help, for humans came running into the park by the dozens, yelling and waving yard tools and baseball bats. The dogs broke apart, the Bull Dogs running one way, the Prairie Dogs another, and Pierre in several directions at once, because all that spinning had addled his brain.

"I must have been out of my mind to join those thugs, even for a minute," Pierre panted when they had left the angry humans behind.

"Bull's not just mean, he's crazy," Dare said. "Just imagine how much the humans will hate him now."

In the days that followed, the dogs found out just how much the humans hated Bull. Wherever Pierre and his friends went—the restaurants, the park, even just walking down the street—humans chased them. Bull had frightened them so badly they were determined to capture any stray dog, even the little ones they had once thought were so cute. Adults wouldn't share their food with the dogs or allow them anywhere near their children. The garbage bins behind the restaurants were fitted with heavy lids.

Pierre thought they had struck it rich one day when he found a pile of chopped meat behind one of the restaurants. Dare, snarling in alarm, drove him and the other two away from it before they could take a bite. She pointed out what they had missed—half a dozen dead mice scattered around the meat. She sniffed it carefully.

"Rat poison," she whispered, and she made Pierre and Mouse lift their legs on it as a warning to other animals. Pierre was shaken by the experience. He had no idea humans could be so evil. Bossy, yes, and dull at times, but this went beyond even the cruelty of the Bull Dogs.

One afternoon Dare took the others to the old grain elevator across the highway. The elevator was a tall, wooden building shaped kind of like a milk carton. The interior was as open and airy as a barn, and smelled like dusty bread. Dare introduced them to her mother, Juju, a fierce little terrier. Battle scars covered her long, wiry body. Her ears were curled by frostbite. She had lost one leg to a train and one eye to a coyote.

"I'm glad to see you have better taste in friends than your brother, Dare," she said gruffly, sizing up Pierre with her single eye. "What's this I hear about you being at war with the Bull Dogs?"

"Aw, nothing we can't handle, Mother."

"Bull's fixed it so we have nowhere to eat!" Mouse burst out. "If it wasn't for gardens and Titan sharing his food with us, we'd starve. Other dogs hide when they see us coming. They know we've been marked by the Bull Dogs. It's only a matter of time before they catch up with us. Either that or the humans will kill us because they think we're all as vicious as the Bull Dogs."

"Why don't you stay here?" Juju suggested. "The humans around here will leave you alone as long as you stay out of their way. They might even feed you."

"No thanks," Dare said firmly. "We can look after ourselves."

"Stubborn pup!" Juju muttered. Pierre agreed.

"Look!" Mew said. Far across the fields, a wolfish shape loped along the horizon. It carried in its jaws some small animal, probably a gopher or prairie dog. The dogs watched until it was out of sight.

"Now there's a dog who doesn't need humans at all," Juju observed. "Maybe you dogs should join him."

"I don't think Wolf would find us a very impressive pack," Pierre said.

Juju took them on a hunting expedition through the elevator. Pierre chased pigeons, Juju and Dare chased rats, Mew chased mice and Mouse chased crickets. No one caught anything, but they had fun trying. The humans ignored them as long as they stayed out of the way of the big trucks that rumbled into the building. Each truck spilled a dusty cascade of grain through a grate in the floor before rolling away for another load. A train pulled up to the elevator and the elevator humans filled some of the cars with grain from a pipe that swung out from the side of the building. The dogs watched the train snake across the golden prairie and dwindle into the distance. If he jumped on it, Pierre wondered, would it take him home? He didn't really want to go back to the kennels, but…

"Let's live at the elevator, Dare," Pierre said that evening in their burrow. "The humans there are friendly. Besides, the Bull Dogs don't go near it, do they?"

"No, but why would you want to live there when it's so much more exciting in town? Besides, you'd have to be crazy to want to live with humans. They can be worse than the Bull Dogs."

"Not all of them. Mr. Abram is kind, and we always have fun with the children. I'm tired of stealing for a living. I want to earn my keep the way your mother does. I want—I want to be around humans again."

Dare sat up and glared at Pierre. "Remind him what it's like, Mouse."

"Back when I was called Chico, my humans kept me mostly in the basement," Mouse whispered. "Often they forgot to let me out. Sometimes it was days before they remembered I was down there. I learned to eat bugs and store extra food in my bed. When they did remember me, they would hit me for making a mess on the floor. And then one day I must have been terribly bad, for they put me in a box, threw me into a ditch and drove away forever."

Pierre touched Mouse's nose with his own to convey his sympathy. "Dogs should be able to choose their own humans, instead of the other way around. That's why I want to live at the elevator. Those humans won't lock us up or hurt us."

"So go, then," Dare snapped. "Who's stopping you?"

"I couldn't go without you. And Mew and Mouse, of course," he added hastily.

The dogs froze as they heard the scrape of claws on gravel and the rustle of weeds overhead. Something larger than themselves was crawling into their burrow. Mouse backed toward the escape tunnel, whining. A low moan came from above, then silence. When nothing appeared, Pierre climbed the tunnel. He peered at the lumpy form silhouetted against the moonlight that shone through the blades of the combine above their burrow.

"It's Old Sam!" he cried.

Old Sam lay on his side in the mouth of the burrow. His sides heaved, his tongue lolled on the ground. His hunter's nose must have tracked them here, but the effort had worn him out. He could barely speak.

"The Water Park..." he gasped. "Tried to bring help...no humans would listen..."

"You came all the way from the old Water Park?" Dare exclaimed. "That's way out in the country! No wonder you're exhausted."

"What happened there, Old Sam?" Pierre asked. "Where's Mr. Abram?" But the old basset hound only laid his head down and panted.

"I'll go to this place and look around," Pierre said. "The rest of you stay with Old Sam."

"That old park is no place for a small dog, especially at night," Dare said.

"I have to find out what's got Old Sam so upset."

"Then I'll come with you," Dare said. "Mouse, Mew, stay here and look after him."

Sometime after the two of them had run off, Old Sam lifted his head and feebly asked Mouse where they had gone.

"The Water Park?" he wheezed in distress. "Oh no! I didn't want them to go there. I only wanted them to fetch help. Don't they know?"

"Know what?" Mouse asked.

"The park is the home territory of the Bull Dogs."

11
The Water Park

PIERRE FOLLOWED DARE across Silvertree, across the highway, and down a dusty gravel road that wound past Juju's elevator and through fields bright with blue moonglow. The town and highway noise faded behind them, leaving only the chirping of crickets, the twittering of field mice and the yips and howls of far away coyotes. A herd of deer crossed the road ahead of them. They stopped to watch the two little dogs run by.

A chain link fence with only one entrance, an open gate, surrounded the Water Park. Pierre and Dare padded through the gate into a ring of yellow light cast by a buzzing lamp. The rest of the park was in shadow.

Before the owners had gone broke and shut it down, this had once been a busy amusement park, complete with rides and concession stands. Tall waterslides had twisted and arched across a wide pool. Now it was one of the spookiest, most dismal places Pierre had ever seen. The skeletal frame of a Ferris wheel creaked in the breeze. The pool was empty except for a layer of mud strewn with stray bits of trash and broken bottles. The slides had been taken apart. At one point the pieces must have been stacked neatly around the pool. Vandals had pulled the stacks apart and scattered the pieces, creating short blue tunnels all across the park.

The painted horses of the rusting merry-go-round seemed ready to spring to life at a moment's notice, but only the rats stirred as the dogs passed by. Pierre put his nose to the weedy grass and tracked Old Sam's scent through the maze of slide tunnels, snorting occasionally to clear his nostrils of a confusing mixture of dog scents. Humans must like to walk their dogs here.

The trail brought the dogs to the top of the hill where the waterslides had once stood. All that stood here now was an easel. The satchel where Mr. Abram kept his art supplies lay open on the ground. His paints and brushes were scattered around the top of the hill. The dogs looked around, but all they could see were the distant lights of Silvertree, and the grain elevator outlined by moonlight. Pierre stared at the painting on the easel. It showed four small dogs standing on a burrow with the prairie stretched out behind them, the sun peeking out from behind an elevator on the horizon. That was why Mr. Abram had come here. He had wanted to paint the sun setting behind the elevator.

"Pierre, look!" Dare cried.

The dogs raced to a small red truck at the bottom of the far side of the hill. Mr. Abram lay on the ground beside the truck. When he saw the dogs he groaned and reached out to them, but his hand fell to the ground and he closed his eyes. They licked his hands and face, but he didn't move.

"We'd better fetch a human," Pierre said. "Stay with him, Dare. I'll run to that farm just over there."

Dare curled up on the old man's chest to keep him warm. "Hurry, Pierre. I don't like humans much, but this one is different."

Pierre ran back the way they had come. When the park gate came into sight, he skidded to a stop. Bull and his pack stood in a row across the entrance. More dogs crept out of hiding places among the old slides and rides until over a dozen dogs stood outlined in the yellow glare of the lamp. Moth shadows flickered across their fur like flames.

Bull stepped forward. "Welcome back, Pierre."

"Get out of my way," Pierre snapped. "Don't you know there's a sick human back there?"

"We know."

Pierre's hackles rose at Bull's smug tone. "What did you do to him?"

"Hey, we never laid a tooth on him. Just chased him and the old hound down the hill. Didn't expect him to keel over like that, but it all worked out. We let the hound go for help, and look who shows up. The timing is perfect."

"What do you mean?"

"The Bull Dogs are moving out, Pierre. We've outgrown Silvertree. It's no longer a challenge for us, and we're too well known among the humans. They're always breathing down our necks."

"Could it be because you're always harassing them?"

"It was the only way to pull my pack together and convince them it's time to move on. Now they have no choice; it's too dangerous for any stray dog to stay in Silvertree. You Prairie Dogs are the only ones too stubborn to accept that."

"Move on to where?"

"The city. I met this husky named Wolf. He used to run with a wolf pack up north, but they drove him out because of his dog blood. Poor guy, he's had a rough deal. Humans hunt him, wolves shun him, even the coyotes will have nothing to do with him. He jumped at the chance to join our pack. He's going to take us across the prairie until we reach a city big enough to suit us. He'll teach us to hunt and survive like wolves along the way."

Pierre nearly laughed at the idea of Bull's small-town bullies comparing themselves to wolves. "Well, Bull, I can't say I'll miss you."

"You won't miss us. You're coming with us."

Pierre backed away. "What?"

"Wolf may get us across the countryside, but we'll need a smart mutt like you to help us survive in the city. That's where you're from, right? That's the real reason I've been trying to get you into my pack. If you hadn't showed up tonight, we would have come after you."

"I don't have time for this, Bull. I have to find a human, or Mr. Abram will die."

"Let him die. He's old. You know what humans do to dogs who grow too old to be useful?"

Pierre hesitated. Dogs seldom spoke of it, but they knew. "I don't care. Old Sam loves Mr. Abram, and so do I."

"That's sweet. Maybe he'll be grateful enough to take you in. You'll have a safe, comfortable life and die old on a cold metal table at the hands of a human. Or you could enjoy the wild freedom of a Bull Dog's life and die fighting, the way animals are meant to do."

"I'd rather die for love than hate."

"That's a noble boast, poodle. Are you willing to back it up?"

The dogs advanced on Pierre, growling. He turned and ran back into the park. The Bull Dogs chased after him, but by the time he got back to Mr. Abram's truck, he had outdistanced them. Dare was still curled up on Mr. Abram's chest. There seemed to be a woman kneeling beside them, touching Mr. Abram's hand. Pierre gave his head a shake, and the woman disappeared.

Pierre dashed up to the terrier. "Dare, is there another way out of the park?"

"When Ratter and I first left home, we wandered into the Water Park looking for food," Dare said. "Some humans chased us. We escaped through an abandoned rabbit burrow that runs under the fence."

She jumped off Mr. Abram. The barking of the Bull Dogs was all the explanation she needed. "Is it safe to leave Mr. Abram here with them?"

"We have no choice. If we don't get away, no one will find him until it's too late. Come on, Dare, let's live up to our pack's name."

This was the most important agility trial of his

life, Pierre thought, as he and Dare darted in and out of the waterslide tunnels. The Bull Dogs couldn't move as swiftly through the tunnels as the two smaller dogs, so they tried to ambush their prey each time they came into the open.

They finally managed to lose their pursuers by ducking into a long tunnel and then backing out of it while their enemies waited for them at the other end. Dare led Pierre to the farthest corner of

the Water Park. Near the fence was a weedy hole in the ground. Dare ducked headfirst into it—and got stuck. Pierre had to pull her out by the tail.

"I forgot," she said sheepishly. "We were only half as big back then."

The sounds of the Bull Dogs grew louder. They had spread out and were carefully searching every inch of the Water Park. It was only a matter of time before they found the two dogs trapped in the corner.

"Pierre, go over the fence."

Pierre looked up at the chain link fence. "It's too high."

"Not for you. Who climbed a tree to get away from Titan?"

"But what about you?"

"Don't worry about me. Running away from big dogs is what I do best. I'll keep the Bull Dogs distracted so they don't know you're gone."

There came a bang and a ripping sound from the top of the waterslide hill. The Bull Dogs had knocked down the easel and were tearing up Mr. Abram's beautiful painting.

Pierre backed up and took a running leap at the fence. Dare yipped in awe at the height he reached before he struck the fence. His paws slipped through the spaces in the links and he had to scrabble to get a grip on the thick wire. With teeth and claws and his strong back legs, he climbed the fence, one slow step at a time, until he crouched unsteadily at the top. The Bull Dogs were approaching fast, but they couldn't see him up here in the dark. He jumped to the ground outside the fence.

Dare ran to the fence. "I knew you could do it!"

"Be careful, Dare." He wanted to say more, but there was no time. They touched noses through the cold wire, then Dare ran back the way they had come. Shortly there came the sounds of dogs yelping in frustration. Dare was leading the Bull Dogs on the chase of their lives.

Pierre looked across the dark field. The warm lights of a farm glowed on the horizon. Pierre stretched into his fastest run. The lazy humans had finally taken a lawn mower to the wheat, leaving prickly golden stubble that rustled with mice and crickets. A rabbit with a red fox close behind flashed past him. The fox gave him a wild, hungry look as their paths crossed.

The quick patter of pursuing feet seemed to follow him even after the fox had passed. He looked over his shoulder. Bearing down on him was a shaggy gray creature with yellow eyes and a white face.

A wide hole suddenly appeared in Pierre's path. It caught his legs and he went somersaulting across the ground. Wolf tripped over him and did the same. Pierre whipped around and ducked into the hole. His nose told him it was the entrance to a badger's sett—the perfect refuge for a burrow-dwelling poodle. The only problem was, halfway down the tunnel he met the badger coming up.

Pierre had never seen a badger before. He had imagined something like a rabbit crossed with a cat. He couldn't see the creature in the dark tunnel, but it was definitely larger than a rabbit and a heck of a lot more ferocious than a cat. The hissing badger lunged at him, gnashing her fangs and slashing at him with long claws. He doubled frantically around and scrambled back up the tunnel. Those wicked claws scratched huge tufts of fur out of his rump as he raced for the surface, yelping.

Wolf had thrust his head into the hole. Pierre nearly leaped into his jaws. His sudden reappearance startled the husky, who jumped back with a snarl. Pierre dodged past him, and a moment later the badger introduced herself to Wolf. The quiet prairie night was shattered by the uproar of a tremendous battle. Pierre didn't stop to look.

He finally reached the edge of the farmyard and slowed down, panting. Then he stopped walking and breathing altogether. It was the farm of the green chickens! Calloway's farm! How much worse could his luck get?

He heard galloping paws behind him again and dashed across the farmyard without stopping to look. He scrambled under the wire fence around the shed of the green chickens. Wolf smashed it to the ground almost before Pierre was clear of it. Poor Calloway would have to fix it again.

There was a wooden ramp leading up to a small opening in the shed. Pierre leaped onto the ramp and shot through the hole. He skidded across a floor covered with straw. The long-tailed birds drowsed on wooden poles above his head, warmed by a red ceiling light that made their green feathers look black. Wolf's head and shoulders appeared in the opening. Blood streaked his white face. Pierre backed into a corner as the husky scrabbled at the floor, snarling in frustration when he couldn't get his wide shoulders through the little entrance. The birds woke shrieking and flapping. Feathers drifted down like green and blue snow.

"You don't have to do this," Pierre cried desperately. "You don't have to take orders from the Bull Dogs."

"I need them," Wolf panted, flinging his body back and forth to work his shoulders through the opening. "The world belongs to humans, and only dogs know how to deal with them."

He lunged forward and cleared the opening. Pierre pressed himself further into the corner. Wolf stalked toward him, his eyes glowing blood-red in the overhead light. The birds fell silent, frozen with terror.

"Bull plans to place you second in command above me. I don't like that. I don't even like the idea of having you along." Clearly, Wolf planned to prevent that.

A door slammed in the distance. Wolf raised his head and listened.

"The farmer comes," he said. "When he has emptied his gun into you, I will kill him, and then slay his birds. The pack will have fresh meat to strengthen us for the journey." The husky forced his way back out of the opening and vanished into the night.

Quick footsteps approached the shed. The door opened, and the glare of a flashlight cut through the haze of dust, straw and feathers. The light fell upon Pierre huddled in the corner, blinding him.

"You again! You have some nerve, you blood-thirsty little mutt!"

Pierre darted back out the small opening. Calloway shouted and juggled his rifle and the flashlight. Pierre raced past the barn, where he could hear the cows murmuring reassurances to their frightened calves, and the angry snorts of the bulls, anxious to get out and charge something. He caught a whiff of Wolf's scent. The big husky was crouched behind the bales of hay piled against the barn.

A shot went off, but it missed. In moments Pierre was in the stubble field, beyond the range of the flashlight. More shots followed, but Calloway wasn't a lucky enough shot to get him in the dark. Pierre drew a deep breath of relief as he heard the farmer curse and fumble in his pockets for more bullets. Then he heard Wolf move out from behind the bales.

Calloway heard running paws and turned around, wondering how the poodle had managed to get behind him. He gasped at the sight of the huge wolf bearing down on him. He struggled to load his gun, but as he backed away he tripped and fell on his back. His gun skidded out of reach. The wolf closed the distance between them in a flash. Calloway flung his arms over his head, knowing it wouldn't help.

Suddenly a small dark blur sailed over his prone body, launching itself at the wolf just as the big animal was about to fall upon its victim.

Calloway stared in disbelief as the wolf exploded into a snarling, twisting fury with the little poodle clamped on its throat. The poodle wouldn't let go, though the wolf's attempts to shake it off flung it around like a dirty rag. With shaking hands, Calloway grabbed his rifle and loaded a single bullet into the chamber. He put the flashlight on the ground and raised the gun to his shoulder. He fired a quick shot. There was a yelp, then silence.

12
Friends in Strange Places

BULL PACED THE ENTRANCE of the Water Park, glaring at the dogs lined up before him. They were exhausted, bruised and whimpering. Mug, the boxer, had an old pail stuck over her head.

"Disgraceful!" the bull terrier growled. "I can't believe you let two little dogs mess you up so bad. I'm ashamed to call you Bull Dogs." The pack whined in shame.

Dare panted cheerfully in her hiding place, deep within a pile of old tires near the gate. Their strong rubbery smell masked her scent. She had outrun and outsmarted the Bull Dogs like one of those clever foxes from Old Sam's hunting stories. They still didn't know Pierre was gone. By now he must be on his way back with help. She just had to stay hidden until he arrived.

She peeked through one of the holes in the old tire. An eye stared back. It belonged to Ratter.

"Don't give me away, Ratter!" she whispered, but the other terrier was already barking the alarm. Instantly she was surrounded by Bull Dogs. Digs, the big retriever, burrowed through the tires and dragged her out by the scruff of her neck. He carried her back to the gate.

Bull glared down at her. "Where's the poodle, Dare?"

"He's on his way back here with humans to help the old man. I'd clear out if I were you."

A series of sharp cracks echoed across the fields from the direction of the farm. A pause, and then another crack, and an agonized yelp. The Bull Dogs jumped nervously. More than one of them had faced the wrong end of a gun at some point.

Bull sighed with true regret. "So much for the poodle. What a waste of a clever dog. That leaves only you to join the pack, Dare. What do you say?"

Dare said nothing. She hung her head in sorrow and whined softly.

"Aw, let her go," Ratter said finally. "We don't need her."

"Are you telling me what to do?" Bull snarled. "Do you challenge me?"

"I challenge you," came a high-pitched bark from behind them.

There were sneezes of astonishment all around as a tiny Chihuahua stepped into the ring of lamplight.

"I'm here to put you straight on a few things, Bull," Mouse said sternly. "First, the Prairie Dogs will never join your pack. Second, you will stay out of Silvertree until this bad reputation you've given all of us blows over. Third, you will stop making trouble for us."

Bull snorted. "You've invited more trouble than you ever dreamed of by talking to me that way, you little rat."

The Bull Dogs started toward Mouse, but froze as a giant copy of the Chihuahua followed him into the light.

"You don't scare us, Titan…" Bull trailed off. Sheba the collie stepped up beside Titan. She was joined by Dare's mother, Juju, and all the strays and house dogs the Prairie Dogs had befriended over the summer. Even Daisy the Yorkshire terrier was there. She trotted over to Mouse and glared coldly at Bull.

"If that's the way you want it," Bull snarled.

The Bull Dogs stood their ground—with the exception of Ratter, who had sneaked away when he saw his mother. The Bull Dogs outnumbered the newcomers, and only Titan outweighed the largest dogs of Bull's pack. Bull's followers and the friends of the Prairie Dogs circled one another, snarling. Dare joined them, shivering in dread. This was going to be a terrible dogfight. Dogs would be maimed and killed.

"Just a minute, please," a small voice piped up, and a pup trotted into the growling mass of dogs.

Dare raced to her side. "Go back to town, Mew. This is no place for you."

"Mew! Mew!" the Bull Dogs mocked, pitching their voices cat-high.

Ignoring them, Mew calmly sat down. "I hope you don't mind, Dare, but I've invited some new members into our pack. I know you don't like animals who aren't dogs, but they're very friendly. They came all this way just to meet Bull."

"Some other time, pup." Bull crouched, preparing to lunge at Titan, to lock his jaws on the Great Dane's throat until he either suffocated or bled to death, as his bullfighting ancestors had been bred to do. "Get out of the way and watch the fur fly."

"There'll be more than fur flying in a minute. Come out, you guys."

Three small animals waddled shyly up to Mew.

Everyone drew close to see what they were, then backed away double fast.

"No!" Bull howled.

Mew's three friends spun around on their dainty paws and raised their bushy black-and-white tails, aiming left, right, and center. Three streams of liquid sprayed across the Bull Dogs. They choked and pawed their burning eyes, staggering blindly in all directions. Soon, maddened by the stench, Bull and the Bull Dogs stumbled out of the park and tore across the fields, howling.

The smell was so rank, even the friends of the Prairie Dogs fled, while Dare barked her thanks after them. Only Dare, Mew, Mouse and the skunks remained. Mouse had fainted at the first sight of the skunks, but the smell woke him quickly.

"That was brave of you, Mouse, to round up so many dogs and stand up to Bull like that," Dare gasped hoarsely, rubbing a paw across her streaming eyes.

"The worst moment was just before we got to the Water Park," Mouse choked. "Titan suddenly turned to me and said, 'I don't actually know how to fight, Mouse. Could you give me a few quick pointers?'"

"I tried to hurry," Mew managed to wheeze in the middle of a coughing fit, "but Pitterpaw, Moonstripe, and Squirt don't run very fast."

Mouse dug a quick hole and buried his nose in it. His voice came out muffled. "I'm sorry we told you not to play with the skunks, Mew. We were wrong. You can make friends with any animal you want, even cats. You know, Dare, those stray cats Mew plays with helped me pass the message along to the other dogs."

Dare wasn't quite ready to be grateful to cats, so she ignored that. "I suppose you'll go back to town now?" she said hopefully to the skunks. Theirs was one scent she did not want to collect.

"Yes, we have to gather our things," Pitterpaw said.

"Mew said we could move in with you," Squirt added. "'There's all kinds of room in the burrow,' she said."

"You won't even know we're there," Moonstripe assured them. She and her two brothers waddled out the gate and down the road.

"I had to say *something* to get them to come all this way," Mew said when the other two turned and glared at her. "Where's Pierre?"

Dare lowered her head. "Pierre…Pierre has gone to the Forever—"

"What is that?" Mouse exclaimed.

A bright light had appeared in the field outside the Water Park. It bounced and weaved through the stubble like a fallen star that had lost its way.

The dogs watched nervously as it drew closer and closer to the park.

Pierre burst out of the darkness and ran through the gate. He dropped the flashlight he had been carrying in his mouth and gasped, "What is that horrendous smell?"

Dare ran to him, yipping and frisking all over him like a giddy pup. Mouse and Mew backed nervously away from her.

"Wolf is dead," Pierre said when the terrier finally calmed down. "The farmer shot him."

"Forget farmers," Dare said. "We'll run back to town to get help for Mr. Abram."

"Actually I did find help," Pierre said. "When the farmer shot Wolf, I stole his flashlight, and he's—"

Calloway stumbled into the lamplight, gun in hand, and staggered to a halt when he saw the four dogs.

"—right behind me," Pierre finished.

* * * * *

Pierre didn't know it, but he was a bit of a celebrity around Silvertree. This was due mainly to Calloway's obsession with catching him. The farmer had made the mistake of complaining about Pierre to a couple of friends, and since then...

"Hey, Calloway, any luck catching the Outlaw

Poodle of Silvertree yet?" the locals jeered when
he stopped by the Gas 'n' Go for coffee.

"You got to watch out for them wild poodles,
Calloway, they'll take your head off!"

"Maybe you should call in the RCMP. You can't
be too careful with these poodles."

They cheered Pierre every time they saw him
and his companions race by with a frustrated
Calloway puffing after them. Bets were placed,
mostly in Pierre's favor.

None of which made Calloway any less determined to put an end to Pierre's freedom. The dog
attack at the playground did a lot to raise his spirits. Maybe now people would take his concerns
seriously and see stray dogs for what they were,
dangerous wild animals that must be destroyed.

To celebrate, he rented "Old Yeller." Now *there*
was a real dog—big, tough, and faithful to the
human race. Those little bird-killing mutts could
learn a thing or two from Old Yeller. It was just
getting to the good part, where the dog takes on
the wolf, when he realised the barking and
snarling he heard was coming not from the TV,
but from his peafowl shed monitor. Something
was at his birds again!

He wasn't surprised to find that wild poodle
among his peafowl again—but what happened
after that was just crazy. First the little poodle

attacked the biggest wolf Calloway had ever seen, then it grabbed his best flashlight and took off with it! At least it was easy enough to follow, bobbing brightly across the field toward the old Water Park, where the rest of the poodle's pack sat waiting.

The dogs took off at the sight of him. He picked up his flashlight and followed, pinching his nose shut against a skunk smell so strong it made his eyes water. He finally cornered them beside an abandoned truck. They sat and looked at him, panting. He lifted the gun regretfully. The gutsy little poodle had saved his life, but Calloway had caught it among his livestock twice now, and the only cure for a killer dog was a quick bullet. Besides, that mad wolf had probably given it rabies, like Old Yeller. He sighted between the poodle's eyes. If he could, he'd get the other dogs too, just to be safe.

The poodle turned its head, and Calloway automatically swung the flashlight to see what it was looking at, and holy crow, there was a man lying on the ground.

A short time later the dogs watched with relief as two paramedics carefully lifted Mr. Abram into the back of an ambulance. A police car drove up slowly, its revolving red and blue lights casting sinister shadows across the park. A woman in a uniform stepped out to speak with Calloway and the paramedics.

"He'll be all right," Pierre assured the others. "The humans will know how to fix him. Where is Old Sam?"

"We left him back at our den," Mouse said.

"Then we'd better get back there and tell him what hap—"

A net fell over the four of them, hauled them into the air and into the back of the police car.

Their days of freedom were over.

13
The End of the Road

THE ANIMAL SHELTER shared a building with the town's only animal clinic. The kennels were clean and warm, and the veterinarian who looked after the dogs smiled often and spoke gently to them. She gave them all a good bath, which only Pierre appreciated—the others had never been bathed before and thought the woman was trying to drown them. Every day she let them run around outside in a fenced yard. Still, it was terrible not to be free, and not to know what had happened to Old Sam and Mr. Abram.

One day the dogs heard the woman speak a familiar name when she picked up the phone.

"I'm sorry, Mr. Calloway, but you can't pick up the poodle just yet," she said. "He has a registration number tattooed in his ear. I'm trying to track down his former owners. We can't release him until we're sure he really is abandoned."

Days dragged by. One morning, nearly a month after the dogs had been brought in, the woman came down with the flu and stayed home.

That was the day Calloway showed up.

"That's the one." Calloway leaned down and smiled into Pierre's kennel. "I'll also take the red terrier, the Chihuahua and that pup."

"I thought you hated these dogs, Mr. Calloway." The man who was filling in for the sick vet glared at him suspiciously. "All summer you kept calling us, demanding that we capture and destroy them. I can't let you have them if they're going to come to harm."

"Oh, they're not for me." Calloway sounded friendly and sincere. "They're for a friend. It's all been arranged. Just ask your supervisor."

"I can't, she's sick." The man shrugged. "Well, we certainly need the room. The shelter's filling up with these skunky strays. Makes it easy to catch them, but phew—what a stench! If you'll follow me into the next room, we'll get some forms filled out and you can take them home."

They left the kennel room, closing the door behind them.

"I think this is it, my friends," Mouse whimpered. "The farmer's come to kill us."

"If this is the end, I should make a confession," Dare said. "I've always liked cats. I only chased them so other dogs wouldn't think I was a sissy."

Pierre paced his kennel. "The end? I don't think so. We've been through too much to give up now."

"Are you going to bite the farmer?" Dare asked eagerly.

Pierre studied the walls of his prison. The kennels were concrete stalls with wire doors, thick walls five feet high—and no roofs.

Pierre gathered his powerful haunches beneath him and leaped. Three tries later, he stood on top of the wall that separated his kennel from Dare's. From up here Pierre could see all the dogs—and they could see him. Bull Dogs, Prairie Dogs and house dogs went wild at the sight of him, barking and jumping and making enough noise to shake down the building.

"Free yourselves, dogs of Silvertree!" Pierre raced back and forth along the top of the kennel walls. The dogs' din rose to an even greater pitch. They leaped and scrabbled at the walls.

"Pierre!" they cheered. "Pierre! Pierre!"

Their caretaker ran back into the room. His jaw dropped at the sight of Pierre standing on top of the kennel wall. He closed the door behind him and

type‌

‌‌‌

GLENDA GOERTZEN

grabbed for the poodle. Pierre darted out of reach.

Leaning against the wall was a pole with a loop of rope on the end, just like the one Calloway had caught Pierre with when he jumped in the creek. The man grabbed it and ran from one end of the kennels to the other, trying to latch onto him. Pierre dodged back and forth along the walls, ducking and skipping to avoid the pole.

The man flung open the kennel doors so he could enter the stalls and get closer to Pierre. The dogs lunged out of their prisons and surrounded him, clinging to his pants legs and growling when he tried to move. He fended them off with his pole and locked himself in an empty kennel. Glaring at Pierre, he gripped his pole like a baseball bat, preparing to swing it at the annoying little poodle and knock him off the wall once and for all.

The door to the kennel room swung open. "Is there a problem?" Calloway asked.

Pierre jumped off the wall, darted between Calloway's legs and through the open door with all the kennel dogs behind him. In the next room, the door to the street had been propped open for fresh air because of the skunkiness of the kennels. By the time Calloway and the other man stumbled outside, there wasn't a dog in sight.

* * * * *

Within a few minutes the Prairie Dogs were standing on the sidewalk in front of Old Sam's house.

"Something's wrong," Dare said.

Pierre knew what she meant. The house looked the way he had felt when his humans left him behind—abandoned. The curtains were closed. No basset hound came baying and galloping to the door when they barked. A woman was pulling dead leaves and wilted flowers from the dirt in front of the house, and a man was pounding a sign into the lawn.

145

"I know what that sign means," Mouse whispered. "It means Old Sam and Mr. Abram have left this house forever."

"The poor old man," Pierre mourned. "What do you think became of Old Sam?"

They went to the museum. The three skunks, now living in their burrow, hadn't seen Old Sam the night the dogs had been captured, nor since then.

"Let's go to the grain elevator," Dare said. "Mother catches all the latest news."

When they reached the highway, Dare let out a sharp howl of shock. The old elevator was gone. Where it had stood was a pile of broken lumber.

Dare ran across the highway. Two cars and a motorcycle nearly skidded into the ditch trying to avoid her. By the time Pierre, Mew and Mouse caught up to her she was circling the mountain of shattered wood, searching frantically for her mother's scent.

"What happened to it?" Pierre gasped.

"The humans knocked it down." A white terrier emerged from the rubble. He sprang onto a cracked timber and looked down at them.

"Where's Mother, Ratter?" Dare cried.

"Gone to live with one of the elevator humans. He took her away just before the humans came and smashed up the elevator with their machines."

"Why did they do that?" Mew asked.

146

"It was too old, I guess. Don't worry about Mother, Dare. I saw her last week. She's fine, except she's worried about you. I saw the humans capture you Prairie Dogs. We thought we'd never see you again."

"Have you seen Old Sam?" Pierre asked.

"Nope. I've seen Bull, though. He's still on the loose, but he's been pretty quiet. Of course, it's hard to cause trouble when the world can smell you coming a mile away. The pack has abandoned him. Didn't like the way he handled things that night at the Water Park. They've given up on the idea of traveling to a city. That run-in with the skunks convinced them they're not ready for a journey through the countryside."

"What about you, Ratter?" Dare asked. "What have you been doing?"

Her brother hung his head. "Hanging around here, mostly. The humans locked up the Water Park."

The four dogs had a quick conference. "You could join us," Dare offered, "if you don't mind sleeping in a badger's sett."

"Really?"

"But you'll have to share it with a few skunks," Mew added. "And if any cats come around you have to be polite to them. That's a rule." Ratter's enthusiasm about his new pack seemed to fade with every word.

147

While Ratter set off to let his mother know Dare was all right, the Prairie Dogs headed back into town. Their last hope for word about Old Sam was the park, where dogs often gathered to exchange news.

* * * * *

With the Water Park closed, his followers gone, and the skunk smell clinging to him, Bull was having a hard time scrounging food and shelter. He had been reduced to hunting gophers, something he had no skill at. He was filthy, hungry and very angry. Any human who tried to catch him now would have been savagely attacked. His only consolation was the knowledge that Pierre and his companions must be dead by now. Most stray dogs who went into the animal shelter never came out. He had lost a few pack members that way.

So when he saw the Prairie Dogs leaving the remains of the elevator, his first reaction was astonishment. Then came the rage. The four dogs who had caused his downfall were running around his town as confident and healthy as could be, while he clung to the bare edge of survival. Snarling, Bull charged past the broken elevator, across the ditch and onto the highway. There would be no negotiations this time, no sneaky tricks or rescues, just a quick death for that clever poodle and those ratty little dogs he called friends.

Bull never saw the truck that hit him. All he knew was a screech and a loud bang, and then a long, long dream where he was still running after the Prairie Dogs, forever chasing them but never quite catching them.

* * * * *

The dogs heard the screech of tires, but didn't stop to look around. They ran all the way to the park, only to falter in disappointment. The park was empty. It was a cool morning in September. Humans were at work, their children were back in their brick kennel, and their dogs were locked up in warm, safe houses. The Prairie Dogs made their way to the empty benches beside the creek.

"Everything's been taken away from us," Pierre said. He shivered in the cold wind, a reminder that the easy days of summer were over and the harsh struggle for winter survival would soon begin.

"We still have our freedom," Dare said.

Pierre lay down under the bench and sighed. "I don't feel free—just lonely."

The other dogs curled up beside him and followed the ancient canine law—when all else fails, take a nap.

Suddenly Pierre opened his eyes and leaped to his feet. Something was horribly wrong. Mew was yelping, snarling and even hissing. He and Dare and Mouse looked around wildly, but they couldn't see her. All they could see was a pair of heavy legs looming over them. It was Calloway. He held Mew in his arms.

"Come on, fellows. Follow me, if you want your little friend back," he coaxed, backing away from them.

"That rotten human!" Dare snarled.

"Take off, you two," Pierre said. "It's me he wants. I'll go with him and try to get Mew back. Go on—no use all of us getting caught."

Dare and Mouse ignored him. The three of them stalked cautiously after Calloway as he carried Mew across the park. He led them to a van idling in a small parking lot. Opening the passenger door, he tossed Mew inside and motioned for the other dogs to follow.

Pierre glanced at Dare and Mouse and saw they were thinking the same thing. If Calloway thought four kidnapped dogs would just quietly sit there while he drove them away to be killed, he had a terrible surprise coming.

Bracing himself for battle, Pierre sprang into the front seat—

—right into the lap of Mr. Abram.

14
The Forever Field

"YOU WERE RIGHT, Mr. Abram," Calloway shouted over the ruckus of five very happy dogs. Old Sam was in the van as well. "They were by the creek, just like you said."

"I knew they'd look for me there," the old man shouted back as he tried to embrace all the dogs at once. He spoke more slowly than before, and his movements were a little stiff, but his eyes were bright, and the gnarled old hands the dogs licked affectionately were strong and steady. In fact, he looked younger, somehow. Maybe it was because the sadness was finally gone from his face. Even Old Sam looked young and spry with joy.

"You dogs saved my life." Mr. Abram's voice was choked with emotion. Calloway rolled his eyes. "I should have taken you in long ago. I'm so sorry I didn't come to visit you at the shelter, but I've been laid up for weeks at my son's house. Mr. Calloway here kindly agreed to help me pick you up. Unfortunately, he underestimated how tricky you little rascals could be! You ran right past me as I waited in the van outside the animal shelter. Didn't you hear Old Sam bark?"

"Are you sure you want all of them?" Calloway said as he started the van and drove out of the parking lot. "They'll be a handful to look after, with you sick and all."

"Not at all. I'm feeling much better. In fact, this incident has done me a lot of good. Made me sit back and come to terms with a few things. When my dear wife passed away last year, I felt my own life was over as well. But as I lay on the ground with death so close, I heard her voice telling me I have some living to do yet. I plan to fill the years I have left with as much enjoyment as my health will allow. I'll start by spending a nice quiet winter in my new home, surrounded by my loyal canine companions."

Calloway snorted. "Quiet? Don't bet on it—not with these mutts around."

Calloway drove them to a small house which

apparently belonged to the man and woman the dogs had seen at Old Sam's house. There was a bit of an uproar at first, because it seemed Mr. Abram hadn't warned his son and daughter-in-law about the new arrivals. However, when Mr. Abram clutched his chest and coughed ominously, the couple choked back their arguments and agreed to let the dogs stay.

Their new home was crowded and the dogs were often ignored for the next several weeks, but one day all that changed. Mr. Abram gathered the dogs into his truck and drove them to the undeveloped property he had visited the morning Pierre had seen him at the cemetery. The house was finished now, complete with paint and shingles and smooth wooden floors in every room. The walls and ceiling of the living room were braced with thick old timbers that made it look like the inside of a tidy barn.

"It smells so familiar," Pierre said as the dogs played hide-and-seek among the stacks of boxes and jumbled furniture. "How can that be? It's brand new."

"It smells like Mother's elevator," Dare said. "It smells like home."

Mr. Abram's son walked through the front door with one last box in his arms. "The house looks great, Dad. I'm glad you finally finished it."

Mr. Abram took the box from his son and opened it. "When your mother died, I just didn't have the heart to complete the house we had planned together. I couldn't bear the thought of living in our house of dreams with only Old Sam for company. But now I realise it's what she would want me to do. Besides, it will hardly be empty, not with these rambunctious youngsters tearing around."

He pulled a parcel out of the box and carefully removed its cloth wrapping. It was another painting of the Prairie Dogs on their burrow. Mr. Abram had painted a new version, even better than the one the Bull Dogs had torn up. He and his son hung it over the fireplace and stepped back to admire it.

"I like the rustic look of the house, Dad. Where did the builders get all this wonderful aged lumber?"

"From that old elevator they knocked down this summer. Didn't cost me a cent."

There was a lot of coming and going of humans in the next few days. Mr. Abram's son and daughter-in-law were nearly always there, fussing over Mr. Abram and helping him unpack his belongings. Friends of Mr. Abram often came by to check on him. A cheerful young woman with gentle hands came by nearly every day to do the cooking and cleaning.

The dogs were confused by all these changes,

but they weren't complaining. Every night they went to sleep in warm baskets in the kitchen. Every morning they enjoyed a fresh breakfast while Mr. Abram sat at the kitchen table, sipping his coffee and reading the paper to them. Mr. Abram's son installed a small flap in the back door so the dogs could come and go as they wished. In the fenced yard they had all the space they needed to run around. As he grew stronger, Mr. Abram took them on long walks through the town and countryside.

"We must have died sometime without noticing," Pierre said one morning as Mr. Abram walked them through a misty field all aglow with sunrise. "This is too wonderful to be the real world. We must be in the Forever Field."

"If this was the Forever Field, we wouldn't have to wear collars," Dare grumbled. Pierre nipped her ear playfully. Dare flew at him and they wrestled until they became so entangled in their leashes it took Mr. Abram several minutes to free them. Lately Pierre found himself inclined to act like a half-grown pup around Dare, but she didn't seem to mind. In fact, sometimes she looked at him in a way that made his heart skip around like a jackrabbit.

Mew went by the name of Mitzy now, because that was what Mr. Abram called her. At first she tried to correct him by mewing at him, but he only looked anxiously at her, so she gave it up. A new name was a small price to pay for her new life.

As for Mouse, to celebrate the start of his new life he decided to give up his addiction to bugs. Of course, now that summer was over there were no bugs to be found, but if there had been, he was pretty sure he could have resisted the temptation.

"He never gets mad at us," Mouse said wonderingly. Mr. Abram occasionally scolded them for delinquent behavior (there was a lot of that, at first) but he never shouted or struck them. When he caught Dare chewing one of his leather shoes he said, "Oh dear, Daredevil's got my sole!" and then laughed and slapped his knee. The dogs suspected a bad joke had been committed.

Mr. Abram often took them to the park, where the dogs would see some of their friends and catch up on the latest news. They learned Dare's mother was still living with one of the elevator humans. Juju enjoyed town life, but she longed for the good old days of hunting rats and chasing trains. There was a rumor the large concrete structure rising near the site of the old elevator was supposed to replace it. Juju hoped the new building would attract enough rats to bring her out of retirement. She was already arranging to have Ratter catch a few to release where the elevator humans could see them.

It was Ratter who told them what had happened to Bull. Ratter was living in the Prairie Dogs' old burrow behind the museum. He had come to appreciate the skunks who shared the burrow with him. The skunky aroma he carried around with him kept him safe from the other Bull Dogs, who now had a terrible phobia of skunks.

Titan and Sheba had become the proud parents of a pair of enormous puppies. Members of the Silvertree police force were showing interest in them.

On a mild sunny day late in October, a motor home pulled up to Mr. Abram's new house. On the side of the vehicle were the words *Princess Priscilla III, l'orgueil de Montréal.* A white poodle jumped onto the dashboard and peered through the windshield as a man and a woman stepped out of the motor home. They squinted through their sunglasses at the old man hard at work in the empty yard, marking off where he would plant a lawn and flower beds next spring. He had already set aside space for a large garden, sadly unaware that he had four incorrigible vegetable bandits living under his roof.

The couple were about to call out to him when five small dogs came galloping around the corner of the house, yipping, yapping and baying. The pair stared at the black poodle, thick with curly, unclipped hair, who chased a red terrier in dizzy circles around the old man, kicking up a flurry of fallen leaves.

"Is that our Pierre?" the woman exclaimed. "How different he looks!"

"He moves like a wild animal, like a fox," the man observed. "It couldn't be Pierre."

The old man had noticed them by now. His face fell into sorrowful lines. He dusted his hands on his knees and limped over to them with the dogs frisking at his heels. When the dogs became aware of the newcomers, their playful barks died away. Pierre hung his head. The others gathered around him, whimpering. The old basset hound looked like it might break into a howl at any moment.

"Thank you so much for rescuing our champion, Mr. Abram." The woman shook his hand. "What a shame the message from the animal shelter took so long to reach us. We've been touring the dog shows across the country for the past two months."

"I'm glad you finally found him," Mr. Abram sighed. "But are you sure this is your dog?"

Now that the pair had a good look at Pierre, they were even less sure than before. This shaggy, rugged mutt didn't at all resemble the refined little champion they had lost only a few months ago. They had to check the tattoo in his ear to be certain.

"Our poor Pierre, he is in terrible shape," the woman exclaimed. "Look, Paul, he has scars everywhere."

"Did you notice a slight limp when he was running, Melissa?" the man said with an anxious frown. "I hope it doesn't slow him down in the competitions."

"Is it true Pierre is a famous show dog?" Mr. Abram asked.

"A champion agility dog," Melissa said proudly. "Watch, we'll show you."

With great enthusiasm, Paul and Melissa transformed Mr. Abram's yard into an obstacle course. The garden stakes became a row of weave poles. With a pile of leftover lumber they built a teeter-totter, an A-frame for climbing, and a set of hurdles. They even dumped the dirt and withered petunias out of an old tire Mr. Abram had been using as a planter and hung it from a branch of the neighbour's tree.

Finally, Paul came over to Pierre and clapped his hands. "Pierre—go!"

Pierre's head snapped up. He took a few steps toward the obstacle course, his muscles quivering with the old eagerness to win.

Then he stopped and sat down. An expression of extreme stupidity settled on his face.

Melissa trotted toward the garden stakes. "Weave, Pierre!"

Pierre yawned.

Paul pointed to the A-frame. "Climb!"

Pierre scratched his ear.

Melissa bounced back and forth over the hurdles. "Over, Pierre, over!"

Pierre sniffed a leaf.

Paul clapped his hands sternly. "Pierre! Tire! Jump through the tire!"

Pierre ate the leaf.

Paul and Melissa shouted commands until they were hoarse, but they had no effect on Pierre. Melissa went so far as to dive through the tire to remind him how it was done, but got stuck halfway through.

"Oh, Paul, he's ruined," she mourned as the two men struggled to pull her free. "He'll never win another competition."

"He's worthless," Paul agreed glumly.

Mr. Abram stiffened. "Now see here—" He stopped, cleared his throat, and went on in a softer tone, "You're quite right. As a show dog, he has no value whatsoever."

Paul shrugged. "I suppose we could use him for breeding."

"And he's a terrible delinquent," Mr. Abram went on. "He and Dare are constantly slipping under the fence and running away together. Of course, they always come back, but when they do they look so pleased with themselves, I am certain they were up to no good."

Paul and Melissa frowned disapprovingly at Dare.

"We'll have to keep him caged up," Melissa said.

"Or," Mr. Abram said, "you could sell him to me."

The pair looked at him in surprise.

"You already have four dogs," Melissa pointed out. "Why would you want another—especially one who has been spoiled by rough living?"

Mr. Abram smiled down at Pierre. "He'll always be a champion in my eyes."

The couple consulted one another. Mr. Abram waited, twisting his cane in his hands.

"We won't sell him," Melissa announced. "We will give him to you, on the condition that if he ever remembers his training, you will contact us."

"Certainly," Mr. Abram lied.

Paul and Melissa bid Pierre a sad farewell and climbed back into their motor home. As it lumbered out of sight, Pierre came to life. He raced through the obstacle course in record time, giving a joyful bark every time he sailed over a hurdle. He gave the tire a kick as he flew through it, making it spin wildly. The other dogs joined him, barking deliriously.

Finally he walked over to Mr. Abram and laid his paws on the man's knees, looking up at him with all the love his eyes could hold. The old gentleman wiped his own eyes and blew his nose loudly in his hanky.

"So the Prairie Dogs are staying together forever," Mouse said. "What a crowd—five dogs in one house!"

"Ah, but not for long," Dare said.

"Why? You're not going to leave, are you?" Mew asked anxiously.

"Not a chance! We've got ourselves a sweet deal here. What I meant was, in a couple of months there will be more than five dogs in this house."

"Really? Who's coming?"

Dare just wagged her tail and looked mysterious.

Mouse glared at her in dismay. "You're planning something crazy, aren't you?"

"I'm tired of adventures," Mew said.

"I, for one, refuse to take part in any wild goings on," Old Sam said firmly. "I much prefer the quiet life."

But Pierre, meeting the tender gleam in Dare's eye, rather thought he might enjoy what was to come.

THE END

ABOUT THE AUTHOR

GLENDA GOERTZEN was born in Morse, Saskatchewan. She decided at an early age to be a writer—in fact, she wrote the first draft of *The Prairie Dogs* when she was in high school. The novel languished in a drawer for many years, while she went to film school and then library school. One day she discovered that the piece of scrap paper she was scribbling on was a page from her long-lost novel. She rewrote it, and the rest is history.

Glenda now lives in Prince Albert, Saskatchewan, but loves to roam the world through her favorite books. She says, "Writers are tour guides, taking readers to places they can't find on their own." Readers will be happy to know that she is already organizing another trip to Silvertree.